DREAM A LITTLE DREAM

DREAM A LITTLE DREAM

Gillian Kaye

Chivers Press • Thorndike Press
Bath, England • Waterville, Maine USA

This Large Print edition is published by Chivers Press, England, and by Thorndike Press, USA.

Published in 2002 in the U.K. by arrangement with the author.

Published in 2002 in the U.S. by arrangement with Jill Kelbrick.

U.K. Hardcover   ISBN 0–7540–4933–7 (Chivers Large Print)
U.K. Softcover   ISBN 0–7540–4934–5 (Camden Large Print)
U.S. Softcover   ISBN 0–7862–4247–7 (Nightingale Series Edition)

The text of this Large Print edition is unabridged.
Other aspects of the book may vary from the original edition.

Set in 16 pt. New Times Roman.

Printed in Great Britain on acid-free paper.

British Library Cataloguing in Publication Data available

Library of Congress Cataloging-in-Publication Data

Kaye, Gillian.
    Dream a little dream / Gillian Kaye.
       p. cm.
    ISBN 0–7862–4247–7 (lg. print : sc : alk. paper)
    1. Large type books. I. Title.
    PR6061.A943 D74 2002
    823'.914—dc21
                           2002024163

CHAPTER ONE

Just as Anna decided that the windscreen wipers could no longer cope with the force of the snow, she felt the front wheels of the car hit something and she came to a sudden and violent halt.

She opened the car door and climbed out into a bitter blizzard of whirling snow to try to see what it was she had hit. Almost blinded, she crept round the bonnet and saw that the obstacle was nothing more than drifting snow at the side of the road.

Back in the car, she breathed a sigh of relief that no damage had been done, but she was filled with dismay that the snow had forced her to a stop on this lonely, country road and that she could go no farther.

She had set off from Leeds just before lunch, and as the sky had darkened and she had got nearer the hilly areas, she had run into snow. At first, it had been no more than a wet sleet, producing a slush on the busy main road and, although driving was not easy, there was no real hindrance to the traffic.

Her mistake had been stopping at a wayside pub for some lunch just after she had turned off the dual carriageway. By the time she resumed her journey down country lanes, they were already white with snow, with conditions

1

worsening every minute. By the time she had reached the turning leading to Stanton-le-Moor, she was driving in exposed moorland, almost unable to see ahead and, more than once, she had thought she would have to give in. But she had kept going, knowing that the village she was heading for was less than ten miles away. Once she dipped down into the dale, and hopefully, out of the snow, she thought that she should have no more problems getting to it.

Quite what she should do next, Anna didn't know. It was January, almost three o'clock in the afternoon and it would soon be dark. She couldn't go any farther in the car and her aunt's house was still at least six miles away.

She thought of her Aunt Beattie who had spent a lifetime in Esterdale. When she had died six months ago, she left her money and her house to Anna.

Anna was Anna Hadlee; twenty-seven years of age, successfully working in Leeds as personal assistant to the director of a marketing company, and living in a very nice flat in Headingley. Anyone seeing her crouched over the steering-wheel of her car would not have guessed that she was a very tall girl with a willowy slenderness; but they would have seen that her long, fair hair framed a face of clear-cut features, determined mouth and large, hazel eyes, usually alight with interest and intelligence, but at this moment, frowning

2

and anxious.

Anna had been satisfied with her job, with her flat and with the friends she had made in Leeds, but when the solicitor had informed her of her inheritance, instantly and without hesitation, she had known that she would move to Esterdale, live in Aunt Beattie's house and make a new life for herself.

She had known the village and the dale all her life, and suddenly the call to forsake city life was irresistible.

Her friends thought she was crazy to contemplate such a move, which made her even more determined. The money that Aunt Beattie had left her would not be enough to live on, but Anna thought long and hard and in the end was excited by her plans. Stanton-le-Moor was a pretty, dales village—the old stone houses and cottages had been built over hundreds of years. Many visitors passed through it during the summer months and sometimes stopped to look at the old church, famous for its brasses. Anna suddenly saw in the village the promise of her new livelihood— she would use Aunt Beattie's money to convert the house into a tea-room and craft shop!

She had seen many such places in the villages of the dales and in the summer season they were both popular and successful. She wouldn't make a fortune, but she was confident that she had enough business sense to be able to cope with such an undertaking, working hard all the summer and relaxing in the dale in the quiet months of the winter.

She had vacated her flat in Leeds that morning and packed her car up with all her possessions. It had been exciting knowing she was on her way to her new life in Stanton-le-Moor—and here she was, stopped by the snow and getting colder every minute. She couldn't see out through the front windscreen, it was a sheet of white. As she shivered, she began to feel worried—she had no food, no hot drink, and with it getting darker every minute, she had to make the decision whether or not to leave the car. Should she stay there for the night and hope for a clearance in the morning, or should she set off on foot in the hope that she would find a house that would give her shelter?

Anna was a level-headed girl, but she was beginning to feel frightened, and as the cold crept through her, she realised that it would be fatal to stay in the car in these conditions all night.

Somewhere in the back of the car was a waterproof cagoul which she used when she went walking. She busied herself by opening first one bag and then another, until she found the cagaul she was looking for. She was dressed in a thick anorak and cords and was wearing a pair of heavy walking shoes that she liked to keep for driving long distances.

She looked out into the gathering gloom

4

and the heavily-falling snow. If she was going to make it on foot she had better move quickly. She struggled with her cagoul and tied a scarf round her head. But once outside, the security that it gave her was immediately blown away by a wickedly cold, northerly wind and the snow which was blowing almost horizontally into her face, stinging her eyes.

She walked down the centre of the country lane in fresh fallen snow. No vehicle had been before her. I must keep going, she said to herself with determination. I'm not too far from the village and I'm off the moor—there must be a house soon.

It was when her legs felt so weary that she felt she could go no farther, and her sodden trousers were freezing cold against her legs, that she thought she could see a gate. The black of the wrought-iron work registered almost subconsciously, but she turned from the road and moved slowly towards it. Surely a gate must mean a dwelling? The snow was still falling so thickly that it blotted out almost everything around, but beyond the gate she could just pick out a row of trees and her heart lifted in hope as she thought she saw a dim flickering light beyond. It must be a house.

Her hand couldn't move the gate, wedged firmly by the weight of the snow and she pushed desperately, shouting out in frustration. At last she managed to move it enough to wriggle through and she found herself on a smooth path of white between trees which appeared to form the straight drive to the house.

As she walked those last steps, her legs trembling as she went, the light became steadier and clearer until she was able to see that it came from a small, long window to one side of a solid front door. It was a long, low cottage rather than a house and never before in her life had Anna been so glad to see the signs of human habitation. Not only was it a house, but it looked as though someone was inside.

Her last thoughts as she raised her hand to the knocker were of hope. As the door opened and she saw a man standing there, she stumbled over the threshold to the sound of his deep, unwelcoming voice.

'What the devil . . .?' she heard him say.

Anna had fallen to the ground but she had not lost consciousness. 'I'm sorry, can you please help me—my car—I'm stranded—'

The door slammed behind her and she felt a strong hand lift her to her feet.

'You'd better come in. What fool game do you think you're playing at being out in this weather?'

Tears sprang to her eyes as she heard the irritable tones. She was inside the house, out of the snow, but was hardly being made welcome.

'Get out of that waterproof—you're

6

dripping snow everywhere. Here, let me help you.' The voice went on half in anger, but its owner was helpful. He pulled the cagoul over her head and helped her off with her damp anorak.

She stood shivering in her sweater and sodden trousers and still the voice continued. 'You'd better get your trousers off, too. Kick your shoes off there and come in by the fire. Wait a minute, I'll fetch you a towel and I suppose you'd better have a pair of my trousers.'

Anna was left standing, cold and bewildered, as she saw him disappear up a handsome, wide staircase. She was in the most beautiful entrance hall she had ever seen, with low beams, old, old furniture of solid oak, surely Jacobean, thick carpet and original watercolours on the walls.

Anna took all this in while the stranger was fetching dry clothing for her. Then he appeared on the stairs again. As he ran down quickly towards her, she knew she was looking at a very tall man. She was tall herself, but he towered above her, with broad shoulders and thick, dark hair flecked with grey. As he looked at her, his eyes were a steely grey with no warmth in them. Had she met him in any other circumstances, she would have been aware only of his good looks and dynamic presence.

He thrust the towel into her hands. 'For

7

goodness' sake, get those trousers off and put the towel round you. Then when you're dry, you can put these on. They'll be miles too big for you, but they're summer ones and you can tuck the legs up easily enough.'

As he was speaking, he led her through the hall into a large living-room. Again she was conscious of luxury, but more than anything, she noticed the warmth. A great log fire was blazing in an ingle-nook fireplace. She stumbled towards it and collapsed thankfully in front of the welcome heat.

There was a complete silence in the room.

Then she looked up at her host and met an expression which could only be described as one of extreme annoyance.

'I'm sorry—' she faltered. 'I was trying to reach Stanton-le-Moor, but I couldn't go any farther. I saw your gate and then the light. Please, don't turn me away.'

'Don't be ridiculous,' he said roughly. 'I've no intention of turning you away. I just don't know what to do with you.'

'Your wife . . .?' she started to say.

'I'm not married. I live here on my own. You'd better get into those trousers and dry your hair. I'll go and get you a hot drink—coffee with some whisky in it. Will that do?'

'Thank you,' she managed to say.

He left her sitting there, feebly trying to pull on the cotton trousers he had given her. They fell about her waist, but she tucked up the bottoms until her bare feet just showed through. I need socks and a belt, she thought, but how can I ask him? He's not very pleased.

She looked around and realised she was in a typical, country cottage, low ceiling with oak beams, white-painted walls, sparsely furnished but with easy chairs and a settee of beautiful design and comfort. All the wood of the furniture was dark, as in the hall and it suited the character of the old house to perfection.

She hardly had time to puzzle about the man on his own in this house, before he had returned from the kitchen with a steaming mug of coffee.

'Thank you.' Was that all she was going to be able to say to this forbidding personality?

'Is there anything else I can get you?' For the first time his tone bordered on the friendly.

She looked at him and hardly dared utter the ridiculous question she had to ask him.

'Have you got a belt? I can't keep these trousers up—and—some socks, please.'

She watched his face and for a single second, thought she imagined a flicker of amusement. But before it had registered, he had turned and gone out of the room again.

He came back with the required items and she managed to make herself look respectable, but he didn't say a word.

Anna sat and looked into the fire. What was going to happen now? It was obvious that she would have to stay here for the night but how could she ask that of this forbidding stranger? She judged him to be about thirty-five years of age, but had the thought that if only he would smile, he would look a lot younger.

The coffee and whisky had warmed her through and given her a little courage. She gave him the mug when he held out his hand for it and was about to explain her situation when he started shooting questions at her.

'Now, perhaps you'll be good enough to tell me how you come to be here. Did you say you had a car?'

She nodded. 'I'm on my way to Stanton-le-Moor, and I've travelled from Leeds today. There was very little snow there and I'm afraid I didn't take much notice of the forecast. It was after lunch when the snow began to get bad—just as I came over the top of the moor into Esterdale. It just got worse and worse until I couldn't see out, then I got stuck in a snowdrift.'

'And you were fool enough to leave your car?' he said scathingly.

Under this attack, Anna found some spirit from somewhere. 'Well, what would you have done?' she said. 'I could have died of hypothermia if I'd stayed in the car all night. I knew I wasn't far from the village and decided to set out on foot. I was hoping to find a house or cottage. And I did,' she said stubbornly.

'And what am I supposed to do about it?'

She looked up and met his eyes. Did he

really mean to sound so aggressive? His expression was still hard and held a certain element of suspicion.

She faltered this time. 'Do you think—could you let me stay the night? I don't mind just sitting by the fire if you haven't got a spare bedroom.'

There was a silence in the room. Anna looked at the flames leaping round the logs, but dared not look up at the man by her side. The atmosphere was taut between them, and she sensed a struggle within him as he tried to find a suitable reply.

His voice was strained when it reached her. 'I have plenty of bedrooms—this is a big house. That's not the problem.' He stopped and she turned to look at him. 'It just so happens that I've had a hard day, I've brought work home, and if we're going to be snowed up for a couple of days, I hardly feel in the mood to have a strange female in the house.'

His abruptness ended in rudeness and Anna jumped up, hardly aware of the comic figure she made in the damp, clinging sweater and the baggy trousers.

'All right then, let's be honest,' her voice was raised, 'I don't want to be marooned here either, particularly with anyone as rude as you are. Show me where the bedroom is and I'll go up there immediately and stay there until there's a thaw. You needn't worry that you'll be bothered by me.'

11

He was standing also, confronting her, now with a guilty look on his face. 'Look, I'm sorry, I didn't mean to sound so inhospitable. If you must know, I was in a foul mood when you arrived on the doorstep, and the state you were in did nothing to improve my temper. Come along, I'll take you to the bedroom and we'll think about a meal.'

He put out a hand to touch her arm in a conciliatory gesture and then exclaimed impatiently. 'Good grief, girl, that sweater is wet through. Why didn't you tell me? I'll have to find you one of mine, though you'll drown in it.'

Anna was forcibly aware of the touch on her arm. It seemed to provide a link of sympathy between them, where before there had been nothing but antipathy. She followed him through the room and back into the hall, climbing the stairs awkwardly with one hand clutching at the trousers and the other holding the bag she had brought with her from the car.

He flung open a door in a long corridor of doors and she looked into a small square room, with a single bed, a dressing-table and what looked like a fitted wardrobe along one wall. At the end of the room was a small, low window with a washbasin underneath it.

'You can have this one,' he said ungraciously. 'The bathroom is next door and I'll fetch an electric blanket. I'd better look for a sweater, too.'

He left her standing there, unable to see out of the window; the light had almost gone and she was looking into a dim, swirling greyness of snow. She crossed the room and closed the pretty, print curtains, wishing to forget the snow. She heaved a trembling sigh—it seemed only that she had left one problem behind and taken on another one.

As she returned from the window, it was to find a pile of sweaters pushed into her arms and an electric blanket thrown on the bed.

'I'll leave you to it,' he said without looking at her. 'You can come down when you want to.'

The door closed sharply and Anna put on the light and sat on the end of the bed. I'm glad I'm in the dry, she said to herself, but I won't leave this room until I'm driven to it. She was thankful to get out of her damp clothes and took off her shirt as well as her sweater. She looked through the pile the stranger had given to her and couldn't help grinning—they all looked far too big for her.

She went next door to the bathroom, and wasn't surprised to find that it was spacious and expensive—shower and bath, and a plant of leafy green on a stand next to the elegant washbasin.

Having a bath and getting a comb through her tangled, fair hair, made Anna feel a little more human and she went back into the bedroom to look for the smallest sweater. It turned out to be a rich, russet colour, which brightened her eyes and hair and made her look younger, though that was the last thing on Anna's mind at the moment. The fact that it came down to her knees didn't worry her either. She was at last beginning to feel warm and comfortable again.

She was also feeling very hungry. Four hours had passed since lunch-time and she had walked a long, difficult road since then. The owner of this beautiful house had said something about a meal, she thought, but she had vowed to stay out of his way . . .

CHAPTER TWO

Half-an-hour passed while Anna lay on the bed and recovered her strength. Then she became aware of cooking smells, and her stomach told her that she would have to go in search of food.

She tiptoed quietly down the stairs in her stockinged feet, pausing to look for her cagoul and shoes; but they had vanished. Then a door somewhere at the back of the house opened and from the smell of frying steak and onions, she gathered that it must be the kitchen.

A moment later, her host appeared.

Anna had no idea that she looked beautiful at that moment; she was used to thinking of herself as quite nice-looking and had no pretensions to beauty. But the dark, warm sweater that almost engulfed her made her look slim and appealing. Her hair was shiny and swinging about her shoulders and her eyes looked large and lost and hesitant.

He came towards her and, to her astonishment, gave a grin.

'You're looking much better,' he said, and his voice had lost its previous edge of hostility. 'That colour suits you. I must apologise for the way I received you. Shall we start again? I've no wish to tell you about my life and I won't ask you about yours—but my name's Paul.'

He held out his hand and she put hers into it thankfully, glad of the truce.

'Anna,' she said simply.

'Pleased to meet you, Anna. I'm cooking us some steak, so come into the kitchen before it burns. You can lay the table if you like.'

Once again, Anna followed him and found herself in the largest kitchen she had ever seen. Paul went over to the modern Aga and as she looked down the long kitchen, she realised that it combined a dining-room for at the other end she could see a pine table and chairs before a tall dresser.

'We'll eat in here,' he said. 'It's less formal than the dining-room—the cutlery's in the drawer of the dresser if you'd like to find what we need.'

Anna enjoyed that meal; Paul opened a

bottle of wine and each sip he took seemed to make him more friendly. She could hardly believe that this was the same man who had given her such a chilly reception on her arrival. They finished off with fruit, biscuits and cheese and Anna insisted on doing the washing up. Paul agreed and he made coffee which they took through into the lounge.

As they sat drinking their coffee, she began to feel relaxed in his company. But it had been a long day.

'I think I'll go up to bed soon,' she said to him. 'I'm suddenly feeling very tired and that lovely meal and the wine has made me feel sleepy.'

He grinned ruefully. 'I must admit, I have you to thank for that. I was in such a bad mood I probably wouldn't have cooked for myself. So in a way, I'm glad you turned up.'

'But you weren't very pleased at the time.' She regretted the words as soon as they were out, but he seemed to take them in good part.

'No, I'm afraid you were the last straw. Because of the weather it had been a difficult day, and on top of that, I had a quarrel with a woman friend of mine making a jealous fuss because she thought I was paying attention to another girl. To have a third girl land on my doorstep felt like persecution! By the way, your cords are on the radiator in the kitchen— they should be dry by tomorrow unless you've got attached to my oversize slacks.'

16

Anna looked at him rather apprehensively. 'Do you think there might be a thaw tomorrow? I want to be on my way.'

He looked at her searchingly. 'Oh, I should have asked—is anyone expecting you—do you want to use the phone?'

She shook her head. 'No, I wasn't expected.'

He said no more but got up and switched on the television. 'The weather forecast will be on in a moment—we'll see what tomorrow's going to bring.'

According to the weatherman, the next day would bring more snow to the north, but rain would spread from the west the following night and there should be a swift thaw in raised temperatures.

Paul looked at Anna. 'It looks as though we won't be able to get your car out tomorrow and you'll have to stay. Do you mind?'

He had spoken quite seriously, but Anna was suddenly shaking with laughter.

He looked at her in bewilderment. 'What have I said?' he asked.

'I'm sorry, Paul. It just struck me as comic that you were asking me if I minded staying here. It should really be the opposite way round—do you mind if I have to stay?'

He grinned. 'I can see your point. I seem to have done an about turn, don't I? Not so long ago I would have been glad to throw you out. To tell the truth, I think you've done me good, taken my mind off my own trivial problems.

And in any case, tomorrow I'll have work to do—I have an office here—so I doubt if you'll see me in the morning. You can lie in till lunchtime if you want to!'

Anna smiled. 'I might do just that,' she said. 'And now if you'll excuse me, I'm ready for some sleep and I'll go on up. Good-night—and thank you, Paul.'

His smile reached his eyes and she felt both thrilled and heartened by their expression. 'Good-night, Anna,' he replied. 'Sleep well.'

Warmth, tiredness, a good meal and a pleasant evening spelled out instant sleep for Anna; she slept soundly and awoke to the brilliant light that only snow can bring.

She pulled back the curtains to find the snow still falling, but steadily and not in the violent gusts of the night before. The garden and view at the back of the house were strange to her, but she could see from the height of some of the shrubs in the border that the snow could be measured in feet rather than inches.

She had slept so soundly and well that she was now feeling bright and full of energy and didn't relish the idea of lying in bed all the morning as she had been invited to do by Paul.

Looking at her watch, she was surprised to see that it was as late as nine o'clock; she felt quite hungry and decided to get dressed and go and forage for some breakfast.

Her cords and jersey had been on the radiator all night and were quite dry, but some quirk of fancy made her put on the bright, wool sweater of Paul's once again. It was very loose but warm and comfortable.

Downstairs she could hear the sound of Paul's voice from behind one of the doors that opened on to the hall. It must be his office, she thought and tiptoed quietly past, making her way to the kitchen.

There she saw at a glance that Paul had cooked bacon and eggs for himself and had left everything out for her—including the washing-up! She gave a grin and set about getting her own breakfast. After she had eaten and cleared up, she made her way to the lounge thinking she would have a go at making the fire, but Paul had been there first and there was already a welcoming warmth and glow from the fireplace. He must have been up early, she thought as she stood in front of a large bookcase looking at his choice of books. There was a lot of travel, biographies, John Le Carré, Len Deighton and the usual range of spy thrillers and detective stories which she would have expected; but also a shelf of Dickens, George Eliot and Trollope which surprised her.

She settled down with a Ruth Rendell she hadn't read, but not without first thinking of the oddness of the situation. Out of the lounge window, she could see the drive which stretched through the front garden to the gate. Her footsteps of the night before had been obliterated by fresh falls of snow; conditions had eased outside, and there was no drifting. She could see across the road to open fields and the distant rise of a whitened moor. There were no other buildings in sight apart from the occasional square and solid, stone barn in the corner of a field.

When Paul eventually came into the room, Anna's heart almost missed a beat. The strained look of the day before had vanished and the smile he gave her had a genuine warmth, almost a sense of pleasure that he had found her sitting there.

'That's as much phoning as I can do for the time being,' he said to her, as he came and stood in front of the fire. 'Shall we have some coffee?'

Anna tried to stifle her curiosity at what his business could possibly be; it was quite obvious that he was not prepared to tell her. He had the look of a business man, or maybe even a solicitor or accountant; she found it intriguing.

They went into the kitchen together. The snow was still falling, but Paul was optimistic about the weather prospects.

'What I suggest is this, Anna. I'll work the rest of the morning and I think that by the time we've had some lunch, the snow will have stopped. This afternoon, I think the drive is the first priority. If we're to get the car out, I'll have to start clearing it.' He looked at her and gave a grin. 'You can help me if you like.'

'Of course I will,' was her rejoinder. 'I couldn't sit here and watch you do all the work; the exercise will do me good. But I hope you're right about the snow stopping—it doesn't look much like it at the moment.'

But Paul was right, and by two o'clock, armed with brooms and a wooden snow clearer, they set to work on the drive. It was a long stretch of white snow which ran down the side of the house as far as the garage in the back garden.

Anna enjoyed that hour. The exercise warmed her and brought a rosy glow to her cheeks. Paul was in good spirits and she felt a sudden sense of close companionship with this man who was virtually a stranger to her. When they reached the front gate, they could see that no vehicle had been along the road and that there was considerable drifting in places where the wind had whipped the snow into sharp, sculptured ridges and peaks.

She looked at it in dismay. 'It'll be days before I can get my car along there,' she said.

'Don't you believe it, we only need a change in temperature and some heavy rain and it will be awash,' was Paul's reply.

She looked up at him and then leaned over the gate. 'You're very optimistic today,' she remarked.

'Yes, I am, aren't I?' He laughed. 'It must be your influence. I suddenly feel young again—I felt terribly old yesterday.'

'Oh, Paul, you can't be a day over thirty.'

'Thirty-five, to be precise, and grey hairs to prove it,' he said.

Anna thought the sprinkling of grey in the raven-black hair was attractive, but she could hardly say so.

They surveyed the results of their efforts and walked round to the back door to take off their boots and jackets. Anna had borrowed some old boots of Paul's cleaning lady and was wearing her cagoul.

In the back porch, he helped her off with the cagoul and laughed at her when her arms got stuck. Then it came off with a rush and Anna overbalanced and fell against him. His arms shot out to steady her then enclosed her to him, fiercely and tightly. Breathless, she looked up into his eyes and saw laughter and some indefinable expression there.

Before she knew what was happening, his mouth was on hers and she was caught in a long embrace. After a second of shock, she went limp against him and her lips readily returned the pressure of his; something deep inside her was telling her that she didn't want this to end, that this was heady pleasure and she longed for it to continue. But at last, Paul lifted his head. He framed her face between his hands and dropped a short light kiss on her forehead.

'Anna,' he whispered. 'I didn't mean that to happen—you seem to have cast a spell over

22

me. Forget it, please forget it.'

He turned and let himself into the kitchen.

Anna stood spellbound for a long moment, unable to think or reason, feeling only the sensation of the kiss and the abruptness of Paul's departure. She had to give herself a shake to bring back a sense of reality, then she bent down and took off her heavy boots.

She felt nervous about going into the kitchen and meeting Paul after what had happened, but she needn't have worried. He was standing at the upright freezer and turned to smile at her as she went in the door.

'Not a lot of choice for dinner, I'm afraid, Anna. There's some fish or more steak. I think we'll have the steak, shall we?'

She nodded her head and went and stood beside him. 'It's not fish weather, is it?' she said rather stupidly, but he seemed to know what she meant.

It was a lively meal and by the end of it, Anna had begun to think she had imagined the episode in the back porch.

That evening, they found they had a lot in common. She looked through his collection of compact discs and found many of her favourites, and they both shared a love of clarinet music. They sat listening to the Mozart clarinet concerto, talking about books and music and avoiding anything that might touch on the personal. He gave her no clues to his identity and it was not until the end of the evening that he suddenly asked her why she was paying a visit to Stanton-le-Moor.

'Have you relatives there, Anna, or some friends?'

She wondered how well he knew the village and had a sudden urge to tell him about Aunt Beattie and of her own plans. She would like to hear his opinion, she thought.

'I had an aunt who lived at Gable End—it's a cottage in the centre of the village. When she died, Aunt Beattie left it to me. Do you know it?' she asked.

'Yes, I do know it. Do you mean Miss Wordsworth was your aunt?'

'Yes,' she replied. 'I've always been very fond of her and have visited her on and off for years. I love the house and I love the village, too.'

'Are you planning to live there, then? It seems a bit off the beaten track for someone of your age.'

Anna hesitated for a moment, then her enthusiasm for her dream overcame her reluctance to tell her plans to a stranger. Sometime during that day, Paul had ceased to be a stranger even though she still knew very little about him.

'I've given up my job in Leeds,' she told him. 'I want to make Gable End into a tea-room and craft shop. There's nothing like that in the village—' She stopped. She had seen him stiffen; he was frowning and his mouth was set in a straight line.

'What's the matter, Paul?' she asked him. 'Don't you think it's a good idea?'

He stood up, then walked to the door.

Turning, he spoke with the same animosity that had been in his manner on her arrival. 'I think it's a terrible idea! It would be disastrous in a place like Stanton-le-Moor, and would destroy the quiet character of the village.' He opened the door. 'I'm going up now, and if I were you, I should forget any ideas you might have for commercialising Stanton-le-Moor—I think you'd meet with a lot of opposition.'

He was gone, and Anna was left sitting staring at the door, unable to believe his words and the swift return to his initial antagonism.

She felt shaken. His reaction to her idea of converting Gable End had been almost violent. He must have some association with the village to have responded in such a way, she said to herself. But Anna possessed a streak of stubbornness, and the thought of opposition to her plan made her all the more determined to carry it out if the house was suitable and she could get planning permission. She couldn't see that planning would be difficult; many moorland and dales villages had tea-shops, and craft and gift shops were to be found everywhere.

She went up to bed slowly and quietly, still thoughtful and not wanting to disturb Paul. She tried to put thoughts of their next meeting far from her mind.

She awoke with a sudden start, long before it was light and to a strange noise. Tensely she listened, then laughed. It was pouring with rain and the noise had been that of snow slipping and sliding off the roof and crashing with a thud into the garden below. She rushed to the window, but could see nothing except the beating rain against the window-panes. Getting back into bed she hugged herself with delight. Thank goodness, she thought, it's thawing and the rain will help clear the snow. I can be on my way.

The next time she woke, it was light and she drew the curtains. It was still raining hard and as she looked out into the garden, she was pleased to see that already there was an edge of green around the white square of the lawn. Shrubs had lost their caps of snow and the trees showed black and bare against the morning sky.

Anna dressed hurriedly, folded up the bed clothes and made sure she had put all her belongings into her bag; the sooner she was able to leave the better.

Downstairs, Paul was in the kitchen.

'It's raining,' she said to him, trying not to sound too excited. 'There's a thaw on.'

'I don't need to be told,' he said shortly, and with a shock she looked at him and wondered where the charming companion of the previous day had gone.

Without a word, she had cereal and coffee. Paul disappeared into the lounge and she could hear him raking out the fire.

Anna washed up, got into her anorak and rolled up her cagoul, stuffing it into her bag. She went towards the lounge.

'I'll be able to reach the car now,' she said to Paul who was crouched over the fire. 'Thank you very much for giving me shelter. It's been very kind of you and I'm sorry I've put you to so much bother.'

He came out into the hall and stood looking at her. 'It wasn't kind—it's not in my nature to be kind. I'm a fool.' With these enigmatic words, he walked towards the front door. 'I'll bring my car down to the front and take you up the lane to your car. I want to see you safely off.'

'No—' she started to protest.

'You've no need to argue—that's what I'm going to do.'

Whatever has happened, she thought, as she stood at the front door looking on to a drive which showed black where they had cleared the snow. The thaw seemed to be a rapid one, as everywhere she could hear running water together with the steady patter of the rain.

A dark-green Jaguar stopped at the door and Anna thought the car was typical of the man. Without saying a word, he held open the passenger door for her and she got into the front seat.

27

At the gate, she looked down the lane and could see that although the snow that was still lying was wet and slushy, the worst of the drifts seemed to have disappeared. Paul drove carefully and to Anna it seemed a long time before her own little car came into view. She couldn't believe she had walked so far, but made no comment. The car was parked at a slant, its front wheels towards the stone wall where she had slid into the drift.

Paul parked alongside and got out at the same time as she did. Anna felt rather nervous as she put the key in the door and slid into the front seat. She tried the engine, which spluttered and her heart sank. She tried once again and suddenly it sprang into life, no worse for its sojourn in the wintry lane. Anna leaned out to Paul and attempted a smile.

'It's going,' she said. 'Thank you, Paul, I'll be all right, now. Goodbye and thank you. I don't suppose we shall meet again.'

'You'd be surprised, Anna,' he replied. 'You might find that you haven't seen the last of me. Be careful how you go down the lane. Goodbye.'

Anna couldn't forget his words and his changed mood as she carefully made her way down the lane. He had changed from the moment she had mentioned the tea-room and she wondered how it could possibly affect him. For the moment, however, she had to forget Paul and concentrate on her driving. The lane

28

was only half its usual width with melting snow still piled high on each side.

As she turned the last bend into the sleepy village, she felt tears come into her eyes, remembering her last visit, when Aunt Beattie had been alive and at Gable End to welcome her.

She drove slowly past the familiar, old houses and cottages set close together at one end of the village, then towards the green and the bridge over the Ester Beck at the other end. Across the bridge, the road went up steeply past the church and the track that led to the moor. The only building on that side of the beck was the beautiful, old house called Windhayes, which had been converted many years ago into a luxury, country-house hotel and restaurant. It stood apart from the village amidst tall trees and in no way spoiled the quiet charm of Stanton which nestled so quietly and so comfortably at the entrance to the dale.

It was at this moment that Anna had her first doubts, but she tried to banish them. A lot of people came through Stanton-le-Moor on their way up Esterdale and many stopped to look at the church. A tea-room would be welcome and crafts were always an attraction when housed in one of the old houses which were part of the village scene. It was not as though she was seeking planning permission to build a new shop and premises which would look out of place amongst the centuries-old buildings.

Gable End was at the wide end of the village, near the bridge, and Anna parked the car on the edge of the green; there was no front garden or garage space to the houses of Stanton-le-Moor. There was very little snow here, but she noticed that there were still patches of ice along the road surrounding the green; the snow might have missed the village but the cold had not.

CHAPTER THREE

Anna sat for a moment, looking at Aunt Beattie's house with new eyes. She had always thought of it as a country cottage, but in fact it was a double-fronted house joined on to cottages on either side. The stone was a warm grey as were all the buildings in Stanton and the roof had stone slates, which were covered with moss in many places and were now showing white in the January morning sky.

With a flutter of excitement, Anna found the bunch of keys that the solicitor had given to her. This was her house now and she knew Aunt Beattie wouldn't want her to mourn any longer—she'd been happy here for many years and would want her niece to follow suit.

She opened the front door with a flourish

30

and as she stepped into the passage she was immediately aware of cold and damp.

Well, after all, it has gone a whole winter without any heat, she thought, but I'll soon get it warm. She peeped into the rooms on either side of the front door, her aunt's sitting-room and dining-room—nothing had changed. Farther along was the kitchen and as she pushed the door open, Anna had a chill sense of foreboding. She could hear an ominous dripping sound, and when she looked into the small room—her kitchen—she almost cried aloud. The floor was swimming with water! White plaster lay in pieces all over the sink; her eyes flew to the ceiling in horror and saw that from the exposed rafters came a steady drip of water.

Even as Anna was looking at the ceiling, another piece of sodden plaster fell with a crash on to the draining-board. Her stunned horror stopped her from panicking. She was sure the solicitor had told her that the water had been turned off and she waded through an inch of water to try the cold tap at the sink. There was a trickle, then nothing.

The cold tank in the loft must have burst, she said to herself. I can get to it through the trap door in the little bedroom.

She ran upstairs into the back room and immediately saw what the problem was—there was water creeping under the airing-cupboard door which she opened hastily. That ceiling was down, too, covering the red plastic jacket of the hot water tank; the water from the cold tank had gushed into the airing cupboard then steadily dripped through into the kitchen.

The worst of the damage was already done, Anna realised. There couldn't be much water left in the water tank, because it was trickling very slowly now. She decided against going up into the loft—she didn't know if it was safe, besides she didn't have a torch in any case. She would have to find a plumber, and her heart plummeted when she realised that the nearest would probably be miles away. She would have to ask a neighbour to recommend one.

While all these thoughts went through her mind, the terrible certainty came to her that the house was not fit to live in. No water, and it might not even be safe to put the electricity on. Had she been a fool to come here? Or had she just been unlucky that the weather had turned so cold?

Walking slowly downstairs again, she didn't go back into the kitchen. There was no way she could face clearing up the water that covered the floor.

She let herself out of the front door and decided to call at the cottage to the left of Gable End. Afterwards, she often wondered why.

As she knocked on the door, she could hear the sound of television or radio within and knew that someone was at home.

The door opened and a very tall woman stood there, not young, but not yet middle-aged; her dark hair was expensively set, she was good-looking and her expression could only be described as haughty.

'Yes?'

The simple word, spoken in a querulous voice, almost unnerved Anna.

'I—I'm sorry to bother you. My name's Anna Hadlee and I was supposed to be moving into Gable End today, but there's been a burst and the kitchen's full of water. I wondered if you could tell me where I can find a plumber?'

Her haughty neighbour's expression didn't alter.

'Do you mean you are Miss Wordsworth's niece?'

'Yes,' Anna replied uncertainly.

'She never did have the pipes properly lagged, but I understood that the water had been turned off—'

Anna interrupted nervously. 'Yes, the water has been turned off. I think it's the cold tank in the loft—the water has come straight down through the airing cupboard into the kitchen. Is there a plumber in Stanton-le-Moor?'

'No, there is not,' came the reply. 'We always get Mr Sleightholme from Kirby Hayton.'

Kirby Hayton was a small, market town about eight miles away. Anna had shopped there many times.

'Thank you very much, Mrs—' She realised that she didn't know the name of this rather unfriendly person who was to be her neighbour.

'My name is Camberley, Marcia Camberley. I hope you are soon able to get fixed up. Goodbye.'

The door was shut with a loud slam and Anna was left standing somewhat bemused. No offer of help, no hint of friendliness—it was not a good start, she thought.

Anna returned to Gable End and searched the telephone directory hoping to find Mr Sleightholme's number, wondering at the same time if the roads were blocked between Kirby Hayton and Stanton-le-Moor. Anna picked up the phone but there was no familiar dialling tone. The line was dead. It was the last straw and she felt tears of frustration and disappointment come into her eyes. Then she stamped her foot and brushed away the wetness.

'I won't give up!' she said to herself, calming down with an effort. 'It's obvious that I'm going to have to do a lot to this house before I can live in it. I'll just take my time and make sure it's all done properly.'

She looked in both the living-rooms. Without Aunt Beattie's cheerful presence, the furniture seemed antiquated and shabby and everywhere was cold and damp; in the grates of the rather ugly, black Victorian fireplaces were the ashes of the last fires that had been lit.

Anna made up her mind quickly. 'While I'm having the tank repaired,' she said aloud, 'I'll have central heating put in; then I'll get the builder to repair the ceilings and after that's all done, I can move in and decorate in my own time.'

So the next problem was to find somewhere to stay. She knew that the only place in the village was Windhayes, the hotel on the way up to the moor. But could she afford it? It had always looked such an exclusive place and it would be at least two or three weeks before the house became habitable.

But she shook her head resolutely. 'I mustn't worry about the money,' she reasoned out loud. 'I've got the inheritance and it will all have to be regarded as part of the expense of starting a new life.'

As she locked the front door and made her way to the car, Anna felt sad and depressed. So far in her new venture, she had met with nothing but difficulties, first, the snow, the mysterious Paul, the burst in the house, and last of all the unfriendly Mrs Camberley and the lack of a phone.

But as she drove over the bridge with the deeper snow on the slope looking very uninviting, she saw with a sense of hope that all the snow had been cleared from the driveway of Windhayes and everything looked well cared for.

The hotel was a beautiful, old building, a typical Georgian, country house, tall and imposing, yet graceful and mellow at the same time; Anna was immediately grateful for the welcome she received when she went inside. She was in a long and elegant entrance hall with a reception desk at one end, but there was no-one in sight; she supposed it must be a very quiet time of year for a country hotel of this type.

As she reached the desk, a girl of her own age and colouring came through the door of what seemed to be the office.

Anna was greeted by a pleasant smile.

'Can I help you?'

'I hope so,' Anna replied with feeling and proceeded to tell the receptionist of her plight and of her need for somewhere to stay for a few weeks that would not be wildly expensive.

'I wondered if you had a small, single room,' she asked.

'All our bedrooms on the first floor are double, en suite rooms, but it so happens that on the third floor, we have two small rooms—they're attic rooms really. We keep them in case we have an overflow of visitors, though most people don't like climbing up two flights of stairs.'

'I wouldn't mind that at all.' Anna laughed.

'They each have a wash-basin and the bathroom is next door.' The pleasant girl was thoughtful. 'I think I could ask the manager for special terms as it's out of season and you will probably need the room for several weeks. Would you like me to do that? Can you give me your name?'

'I'd be most grateful,' Anna said. 'I'm Anna Hadlee and my aunt was Miss Wordsworth who lived at Gable End in the village.'

'Oh, we all knew Miss Wordsworth—she was a great character. So it's her house you are moving into?'

'Yes,' Anna said ruefully. 'When I've succeeded in getting it straight. I must have central heating put in. I don't know how she managed with coal fires and no heating at all upstairs.' She shuddered.

The receptionist laughed. 'I think that generation were brought up to much harder ways. We seem to want a softer and more comfortable life, don't we? I'll go and look for Michael—he's the manager. I'm Linda Milner, by the way.'

She came back a few minutes later with a pleasant-looking young man in his early thirties. He had sandy hair and blue eyes and Anna liked him immediately.

'Miss Hadlee,' he said, holding out his hand in greeting. 'We would be only too pleased to help you out if you think you can manage with the small room on the top floor.'

They discussed terms, which to Anna's relief were quite reasonable and would include an evening meal. He shook hands with her again and asked Linda to show her up to the room.

As they walked up through the hotel, Anna had the feeling of quiet comfort which was at the same time luxurious. On the first landing, even at this time of year, there were flowers arranged attractively in a gleaming, brass bowl on a long, ash chest, and the second stairway, narrower, was thickly carpeted.

She was delighted with her room; it was small, but did have a comfortable easy chair which pleased her. It was furnished in soft greys and pinks and the window looked out on to the back garden, with the moor rising behind it.

Anna turned to Linda. 'It's lovely,' she said. 'And it will suit me very nicely for a few weeks. I have a lot of household goods with me, but I can take them back to Gable End. I'll only bring in what I need. I think I'll go and unload now.' She was eager and relieved to have found somewhere comfortable to stay, but suddenly remembered—'Oh, and is there a phone downstairs? I must get hold of a plumber.'

'Yes, there's a pay-phone by the restaurant; the double rooms have their own phone and television, but I'm afraid this room doesn't have those luxuries.'

'That's all right. I'm told there's a Mr Sleightholme in Kirby Hayton, but, of course, he might not be there in the middle of the day. Perhaps I'll move in and phone him this evening.' Anna walked downstairs again with Linda and in a very short space of time, they had carried her case and bags up to her room. The rain had stopped but the air felt quite mild after the arctic conditions of the last few days and there was the sound of rushing water everywhere.

By the time Anna had eaten her evening meal and had contacted the plumber, she was feeling much happier. He had agreed to meet her at the house the next afternoon, and had told her that although he didn't do central heating himself, he worked alongside a firm that did and he would bring someone with him to give her an estimate. He didn't expect them to be busy at this time of year as not many people wanted central heating put in during the winter.

*   *   *

Putting the house in order took a lot of hard work. It took Anna a whole day to mop up the kitchen once the new cold tank had been put in and then she had to clear up the mess made by the fallen plaster.

She contacted a local builder who came to repair the ceilings and painted the kitchen at the same time. As these jobs were completed, Anna began to feel more cheerful and hopeful.

She busily sorted through the furniture, reserving the good pieces and piling up everything she didn't want, waiting for a second-hand furniture dealer to come from Kirby Hayton.

By the end of the first week, she had water, the electricity was checked and pronounced safe, and the phone had been reconnected. The central heating people were due the following week and that would mean more chaos, but she didn't mind—at last she felt she was getting somewhere. She was comfortable at Windhayes and had made a good friend of Linda who lived on the edge of the village.

The hotel was busier than she had thought it would be as they offered weekend breaks in the winter and these seemed to be popular. Linda worked odd hours, but didn't seem to mind; she helped with the typing and accounts as well as her reception duties and always seemed to be busy. The two girls usually had coffee together in the middle of the morning and Anna had taken Linda to see Gable End.

During this time, Anna was often to think of the time she had been stranded in the snow and naturally, of Paul. He had aroused not only curiosity within her, for she found that she could not forget the brief, physical contact of their kiss and the longing it had stirred within her. While she had been stricken and upset by his hostility before their parting there was much in him that had been attractive to her and she wished many times that she might meet him again; he was the kind of person not to be forgotten easily.

Almost three weeks to the day after arriving at Stanton-le-Moor, Anna was ready to move into her house. The heating was installed and working, and the building had lost its damp feeling. She had given a good deal of thought to the decorating and decided to live in one of the bedrooms while she worked her way through the rest of the house. Fortunately, the walls had been left white, preserving the old atmosphere of the house and the wooden beams were all well preserved. She was glad because she had the feeling that wallpaper wouldn't suit the character of the place.

On her last evening at the hotel, Linda was free so the two girls drove to the neighbouring village of Huckleby to have a meal out at The Plough.

It was a tiny inn at the end of the village, renowned for its good food and a favourite place for visitors to Esterdale and for the residents of Kirby Hayton.

Being a Monday and still only February, the inn was quiet and Anna and Linda could relax in comfort.

'I've got used to seeing you around, Anna,' Linda was saying. 'It's going to seem strange without you.'

'Perhaps we'll be able to have the occasional evening out,' Anna replied. 'I'm not going to be far away, after all.'

Linda looked at her friend. 'I don't want to seem inquisitive,' she said suddenly, 'but are you going to get a job or something? I know you said you had a good job in Leeds, and I wondered what you were planning to do.'

Anna felt a momentary hesitation. The last person to whom she had mentioned her idea had been Paul and the effect had been devastating. She was wondering now what Linda would think and thought perhaps it would be a good idea to sound her out—she was a local person and would know local opinion.

She spoke slowly. 'When I've got the house straight,' she said, 'I'm going to apply for planning permission to open a small tea-room and craft shop—I thought it might be a nice idea in a village like Stanton-le-Moor.'

Linda looked startled and for a moment was silent.

'What do you think of the idea?' Anna asked. 'I would value your opinion, Linda.'

'I don't know what to say,' Linda replied. 'I've often thought that we could do with a tea-room. A lot of visitors go through on their way to Esterdale and people always like a craft shop. I'm not against it myself—' She hesitated and Anna leaned towards her.

'But what, Linda?' she prompted. 'Don't be afraid to tell me.'

'Well, a lot of local people are against the

idea of commercialising the village. It hasn't changed for hundreds of years and they think it should be left as it is. People from the south have tried to buy properties for holiday cottages in the past but there was so much opposition, that somehow or another the purchases have never succeeded. I'm sorry, Anna, I'm not trying to put you off but I think you would be up against it.'

'Someone else said just the same,' Anna said, thoughtfully. 'I'm not really surprised at what you've told me. But one small tea-room with a craft shop attached is hardly commercialisation. I can't see that it would spoil the village—visitors stop to look at the church, in any case.'

'Yes, but once planning permission has been given for one venture, it opens the door for other things,' Linda pointed out. 'I think that's what local people are afraid of. And I know one person who would be against it—Mr Buxton.'

'Mr Buxton? Who is he?' Anna asked her.

'He owns the hotel.'

Anna looked puzzled. 'But I thought Michael was the owner?'

Linda shook her head. 'No, he's only the manager. It's one of a chain owned by Mr Buxton and I know he's very keen to keep the hotel select and quiet and not to have the peace of the village spoiled by day trippers.'

'So I'd be up against Mr Buxton, would I?'

Anna said grimly. 'Has he a lot of influence in the village?'

'Yes, he has. He's on the District Council and he lives locally, too—only about seven or eight miles out of Stanton. He doesn't always win, though. Last year Gerry Pearson opened the riding stables and Mr Buxton tried to get it stopped, but it's not really in the village so he wasn't very successful. Gerry did very well last summer. Do you know him?'

Anna shook her head. 'No. I've passed the stables and I may have seen him, but I've never met him.'

'You'd like him. He's a bit older than we are, but he's great fun.'

Anna looked at Linda and wondered if she sensed a romance. She had thought these past weeks that Linda was more than a little keen on Michael at the hotel, but he seemed to see Linda as just another of his staff.

'You've given me a lot to think about,' she said to Linda. 'Thanks for being so honest. I'm not put off and I'm prepared to fight. I know I could make a success of it and the house lends itself to what I want to do. I can make a tea-room out of the dining-room and knock a door through into the kitchen—I may even enlarge the kitchen, if I can get permission. Then on the other side of the front door, there's a nice, big room which would be ideal for crafts. I don't mean cheap, gifty things, Linda, but perhaps I can find some local pottery and woollens, that kind of thing.'

'It sounds very nice, Anna, and I certainly wish you all the best, but don't say I didn't warn you.'

The conversation turned to other things then and the evening passed pleasantly and happily.

CHAPTER FOUR

The next morning, as soon as breakfast was over, Anna packed her clothes and Linda helped her to carry her bags and cases to the car.

Moments later, Anna was at the reception desk concentrating on writing out a cheque to settle her account and was hardly aware that the front door had opened and that someone had come into the entrance hall.

The sound of Linda's voice interrupted her thoughts.

'Why, good-morning, Mr Buxton,' she said, in surprise and pleasure.

At the sound of the name, Anna glanced up quickly and turned to look at the man who was walking towards them.

'Good-morning, Linda,' he said and he turned to Anna. 'Well, Anna, so we meet again?'

Anna found herself looking up into amused

and smiling eyes.

It was Paul!

Linda looked from Paul Buxton to Anna in astonishment. 'But how . . . ?' she started to say.

Paul was holding Anna by the hand and seemed genuinely pleased to see her. Anna was still recovering from shock, as the truth dawned on her—the Paul of the snow-storm and the Mr Buxton of the hotel were one and the same person. She was remembering, too, what Linda had told her about Paul Buxton's attitude to changes in the village. She felt tongue-tied and was glad of Linda's delighted amusement.

'Anna's been staying here for three weeks while her house was made fit to live in—she's moving in there today.'

Paul looked at Anna. 'And did you tell Linda about getting stranded on your way to Stanton-le-Moor, Anna?'

Anna flushed and looked at Linda. 'Do you remember, I told you how my car was stuck in the snow and I sheltered at a house just outside of the village? Well, it was Paul's house. I had no idea that his name was Buxton or that he had anything to do with the hotel. I haven't seen him about the hotel, have I?'

Linda shook her head. 'Windhayes is one of a chain, Anna. I thought you realised that. It's a Heron hotel and Mr Buxton owns them all— he just gets round to us every so often.'

Anna stared at Paul. 'Do you mean you own all the Heron hotels? I thought they were just a hotel association and that Windhayes was one of them; I didn't realise they were all owned by the same person.' She spoke almost accusingly. 'You can't possibly own them all—there are so many of them.'

He seemed to delight in her discomfiture. 'I'm afraid I do, Anna. Sorry to give you such a shock. Now you know why I was so busy that morning when you were staying with me. I was snowed in and guessed that half the hotels would be, too—I could only contact them by phone. Fortunately, I've got a staff of excellent managers, like Michael here. It makes my job very easy.'

Anna was still dazed, but creeping back into her conscious memory was the thought of Gable End and the dreams she had for it. Standing before her was not the charming saviour from the snow, but her arch-enemy—the person who had it in his power to destroy all she was planning to do.

Apart from that, she found herself wishing that he was a little less good-looking and that his grey eyes were not so alive and magnetic. Her senses were a conflicting clash of memories—the angry Paul Buxton of her arrival at his home—the companionable Paul with whom she had found so much in common—and last of all, the bitterly antagonistic Paul who had called her idea for

47

Gable End 'terrible'.

She spoke stiffly. 'I haven't forgotten your kindness, Paul—nor have I forgotten that you were opposed to my ideas for Gable End. I now understand from Linda that you have considerable influence in the area and would do your best to stop me. I must tell you that I have no intention of being stopped. I have already started converting the house and hope to open the tea-room by the early summer. I'm leaving Windhayes today, so I'll bid you goodbye. Goodbye, Linda, I've left my cheque on the desk.'

Without looking at either of them, she walked down the hall and out of the front door and would have slammed it behind her but for the fact that it was constructed with a very strong spring.

Behind her, Paul Buxton looked at Linda and grinned. 'I seem to have upset Anna. I don't even know her surname—what is it, Linda?'

'It's Hadlee. She's the niece of Miss Wordsworth who died last year and lived in that house in the village all her life.'

Paul was thoughtful. 'And have you been encouraging Miss Hadlee in her folly, by any chance? You seem to be on friendly terms with her.'

'No, Mr Buxton, I haven't encouraged her. In fact, I told her you probably wouldn't approve. But at the same time, I can't help thinking it might not be a bad idea. The house is in just the right position for a tea-room—it wouldn't seem out of place.'

Paul groaned. 'Not you, too,' he said. 'I won't have the village spoiled by tourists. I shall fight her all the way—even if I do think she's a beauty.'

Linda looked at him, startled by this unexpected remark; there was a question in her eyes but she hid it as she spoke. 'I think she's a very determined girl, Mr Buxton.'

'I can be determined, too,' he said shortly. 'In fact, I'm going to go and tell her so and have a look at this damned house of hers. Where is it?'

Linda's eyes widened. 'It's on the green, Mr Buxton. It's next door to—'

But he had gone and she had to turn to a bewildered Michael who was watching his employer disappearing out of the front door.

Anne had just taken her first case from the boot when Paul's car drew up alongside her. He jumped out and took the case from her.

'I'll carry it,' he said.

Anna was not pleased and did not sound pleased. 'I can manage very well without your help, Mr Buxton. In fact, I don't know what you're doing here. I've no wish to speak to you.'

'So we're to be formal, are we, Anna? I want to speak to you and I want to see this house of yours.' He was already walking towards the front door carrying two of the cases, and she looked on helplessly and put the key in the lock.

'How did you know where to find me?' she asked waspishly as they stepped into the hall.

'I know Gable End. It so happens that a good friend of mine lives next door.'

'Mrs Camberley?' she asked, astonished.

'Yes, Mrs Camberley,' and that was all he said.

He was glancing around him, opening doors and looking into the rooms; Anna did not seem to be able to find the words to stop him.

'Hmm,' he remarked. 'The rooms are bigger than I had imagined they would be, but I can see you've got a lot of clearing out to do, not to mention the decoration. It all looks rather dark and damp.'

'It may be dark, but it's not damp,' she said, sharply, 'I've had central heating put in and the house has been drying out for weeks. There was a burst when I arrived here.' She ended up with a rush of confidence.

He looked at her. 'So that's why you have been staying at the hotel. I trust you were comfortable?'

'Yes, I was, thank you.'

He was still looking about him and Anna realised she was tensing herself and waiting for a critical remark.

It came with some force. 'So one of these rooms is to be a tea-room, and the other a shop to sell crafts. Is that your little dream, Miss Hadlee?'

'Yes, it is,' she said hotly. 'And it's not just a dream. If you must know, I've already applied for planning permission and have begun enquiring about shopfitters. The decorating I shall do myself in these next few weeks.'

'You sound very confident that you'll get your planning permission.'

'I don't see why I shouldn't be. There's a great move on the part of the National Park to promote the tourist industry and I know of a lot of villages which have successfully opened small museums and galleries, and where the tea-room and the craft shop are useful adjuncts.'

'And have you seen any of those villages recently, Anna?'

She looked at him; what was he trying to say? But she had to be honest.

'No, it's several years since I had a tour round,' she answered him.

'I thought as much,' he said, 'Perhaps one day I will take you on a "tour round" as you put it.'

Anna still felt tense and angry. 'I've no wish for your help, Mr Buxton, and certainly don't welcome your interference in my affairs.'

He looked her straight in the eyes. 'The moment that a planning notice goes up in front of your house, Miss Hadlee, you will invite opposition to your plans. And I'm telling

51

you now, being frank with you, I shall lead that opposition.'

She almost cried out as she interrupted him. 'But what have you got against it? I've no intention of spoiling the village!'

He spoke stiffly. 'You might not have that intention, but you would open a floodgate. And as long as I have anything to do with the village, I'm not going to let Stanton-le-Moor be to Esterdale what Hutton-le-Hole is to the North Yorkshire Moors. I shall fight you all the way, Miss Anna Hadlee.'

Anna really did see red that time. 'You are a beast, Paul Buxton. Thinking you own not just the hotel, but the whole village. Well, I shall fight, too, and I can tell you I can be very stubborn and determined. I shall win. In the meantime, I'd be glad if you would leave me in peace so that I can get unpacked. I've no wish to see you again as long as I live.'

He looked at her bright eyes. 'The feeling is mutual, Anna—almost.' And he leaned forward and touched her lips with his, softly and briefly and with a meaning that was hidden from her. Anna felt the stir that his touch could give, a trembling, expectant feeling. Then she watched him turn away from her, let himself out of the front door and seconds later, she heard the roar of the Jaguar as it sped through the village back to the hotel.

Anna stood in the shabby, old house, trying to fight back the tears that his words and his final action had brought to her. I won't let him get me down, she said to herself. He's the most self-opinionated man I've ever met and I loathe him—then she had to add the same word as he had—almost.

She spurred herself into action, unpacking the cases in the one decent bedroom that had been Aunt Beattie's; the furniture was antiquated but it had pretty wallpaper and curtains, and would suit her purposes adequately for the time being.

During the next few weeks, Anna thought she had never worked so hard in her life, but she enjoyed herself. She got rid of the old, useless furniture; she painted every room and while she was making things good, she had the beams treated; the smell was awful but she opened the windows to air the room and learned to live with it.

She and Linda met once a week and both enjoyed this new friendship. Linda talked a lot about Michael but she didn't mention Paul Buxton again and Anna didn't ask about him. She hadn't seen anything more of him. With a contrariness to her feelings, she was glad about this, yet she knew there was part of her that wanted to see him—even if it was to have another quarrel with him.

By the end of March, with Easter almost upon them, she had done as much as she could do and the authorities were meeting to consider her planning application, though no notice had gone up outside. She learned from Linda that there was considerable talk about Gable End in the village—she had even heard that one of the residents was getting up a petition to try to stop the plan.

Anna had seen nothing more of her haughty neighbour, and she hadn't found any of the villagers she had met particularly friendly either.

But she did make one friend, and he turned up just when she was beginning to feel she had done all she had to do and was waiting nervously to hear whether she could go ahead with her tea-room.

It happened to be April first, with Easter a week away and Anna was cleaning the windows at the front of the house when a Land-Rover drew up and a man jumped out of it and came up to her.

'Hi, there!' he said, with a broad grin. 'I thought I'd stop and introduce myself. I'm Gerry Pearson from the riding stables.'

Anna found herself looking into bright, blue eyes in a brown, weather-beaten face. He was not a tall man, but his strong physique gave the impression of boundless energy. His hair was a light brown, but not fair, and Anna could not guess his age; he looked about forty but could have been younger. She shook hands with him

'I'm Anna Hadlee,' she said to him. 'I'm very pleased to meet you. I've heard about you. Will you come in and have a coffee with me? I'm feeling in need of moral support at the moment and perhaps you're the person to give it to me.'

He laughed. 'I'd love to,' he said. 'I think I know what you're going to ask.'

Over coffee, Anna couldn't stop talking. Gerry Pearson's open, friendly face invited confidence and she told him how edgy she was feeling about the planning application. Did he know about it?

'I think everyone in the village knows,' he replied. 'And you know you're going to be faced with opposition, don't you?'

'Yes. I know that. You did, too, didn't you? From Mr Buxton.'

'I did indeed. I'm afraid he's against any development in the village—thinks it'll spoil the select quality of his hotel, I suppose. But you see, Anna, my riding stables aren't actually in the village and I won my case. You're in a different position. It's a tea-room you want to open, isn't it?'

'Yes, that's right, and a craft shop. I thought they'd do quite well in a place like this, and it's not unusual to find them in villages in the dales. What do you think, Mr Pearson?'

'Gerry.'

She smiled. 'Tell me what you think, Gerry.'

He seemed to have no hesitation. 'I'm on your side absolutely, bring a bit of life to the place; a tea-room will help the riding-school and vice versa.'

Anna gave him a broad smile. 'You're the first person who's been in favour. Even my friend, Linda, from the hotel—she's keen on the idea, but she's very pessimistic about it.'

'Don't you look on the black side—there are lots of people who want to promote the dales. I've got to know one or two people on the council. I'll nobble them for you if you like.'

'Oh, you are good. You've cheered me up already. Thank you so much for stopping by.' Anna felt as though she could have hugged him.

He put out a hand and grasped her arm. 'It's a pleasure,' he said. 'And now we've met, how about coming out to dinner with me one evening? I know one or two small pubs that do excellent food.'

Anna smiled. 'I'd love to, Gerry,' she said. 'And thank you.'

'Don't mention it. I think it'll have to be after Easter because it's a busy time for me, but I won't forget—I'll give you a ring to fix it up.'

A few days later, the first of the anonymous letters arrived. It made Anna feel sick and shaky. An envelope was pushed through her letter-box late one evening after dark, and she picked it up feeling very curious. The writing was spidery and rather shaky as though it had been written by an elderly person. The inscription was simple, just Miss A. Hadlee, and no address. She took it into the living-room and opened it and when she saw the single sheet of paper, she stared in disbelief.

You think you are going to spoil our village.
You are wrong—we will stop you.

It was not hand-written, or even typed, but was composed of words cut out from a newspaper stuck on to a plain piece of white paper.

Anna's hands shook as she stared at the words. Who could possibly have sent this? She knew that feelings were aroused in Stanton-le-Moor, but she had never imagined that anyone could have disliked her scheme so much that they would have sent an anonymous letter.

She was unhappy that night and could not sleep, the words of the letter repeating themselves endlessly in her mind. First thing the next morning, she got up and decided to burn the letter—that was the best way of dealing with such things, she thought.

She spent Easter quietly and attended the morning service at the church on Easter Day. People gathered outside the church after the service but there was no-one she knew and not one person made any move to speak to her. She even felt as though they were looking at her and saying that's the young woman who wants to open the tea-room and it was forced into her mind rather sorrowfully that perhaps amongst them was the person who had sent the anonymous letter.

When she got home, she felt like crying, but had her mind taken off the incident by the sight of Paul Buxton's car drawing up on the green.

For a moment, Anna's heart gave a leap, almost as though she would welcome a visit from him and forgetting the harsh words of their last meeting. Then to her astonishment, she saw him walk up to the cottage next door and let himself into Mrs Camberley's house.

Paul and Marcia Camberley? Surely not, she thought. She must be years older than him. She remembered he had told her that he knew her neighbour. Then she realised she was being inquisitive and concentrated the rest of the day on getting her meal and going for a walk in the afternoon.

The next day, Paul's car was on the green again and it disturbed Anna to see it there. It was the Bank Holiday Monday and she had decided to stay indoors. There would be crowds of people everywhere, she thought, particularly as it was fine and sunny.

Even as the thought came to her, she realised with a blinding flash that she was guilty of double standards. She didn't want to go out because of the crowds in the dale, yet what she was planning to do would bring those same crowds to her doorstep. 'I'm getting confused,' she said to herself, and the memory of the letter didn't help. 'I need to talk to someone. Gerry will be busy today, but I'll go and see him tomorrow.'

The last person she had expected to see was Paul Buxton, but at about three o'clock that afternoon, there was a knock on her front door and when she opened it, it was a shock to find him standing there.

'Paul!' His name escaped her involuntarily.

'Can I come in, Anna? I want to ask you something.' He sounded friendly and pleasant.

She felt flustered but led him into the living-room and listened to what he had to say.

'I was planning to drive over to Hatton Stacy and wondered if you'd like to come? I don't think you've been there yet.'

She knew that Hatton Stacy was a pretty village farther up the dale and she was curious to see it. But it was not words of acceptance that escaped her.

'But what about Mrs Camberley?' Anna could have bitten her tongue out as she saw a deep frown come between his eyes.

'What about Mrs Camberley?' he replied caustically. 'I didn't think you'd be the type to go in for spying behind the curtains. So you've seen me visiting Marcia? She's an old friend of mine—I told you that, didn't I?'

'I'm sorry, Mr Buxton,' she said in a small voice. 'I just happened to see your car draw up yesterday and to tell you the truth I thought you were coming here.'

He gave a shout of laughter. 'And I hope you were disappointed, Anna.'

How hateful he was, she thought, and said nothing.

'But please come this afternoon,' he continued. 'Marcia and I were going to ask you but she has one of her nervous headaches and doesn't want to go out. I won't be here again for a little while, so, please, say you'll come.'

Anna gave in suddenly; she might find the man hateful, but in a contrary kind of way, she also found him irresistible and she was glad of the invitation.

'OK, I'll come. I'll just get ready—it won't take me a minute.'

'And no more Mr Buxton?' he asked in a teasing manner.

'No—Paul.' She smiled a little shyly and hurried upstairs.

In a short while, they had joined a slow stream of ears making their way up the dale.

'Everybody's out today in the sunshine,' she remarked.

'Yes, the first Bank Holiday of the year always brings everyone out,' he remarked. 'And yet, you know, Anna, if you take a step down any of these lanes or tracks and walk up on to the moor, you won't see a soul.'

She glanced up at him. 'You like solitude, Paul?'

'Yes, I must admit, I do. In my type of job, it's a relief to be on your own once in a while with nothing but heather beneath your feet and a clear sky above.'

She wondered at his words and was silent; things were tugging her all ways today, she thought, for she, too enjoyed a solitary walk high up on the moors but she hadn't expected to share the feeling with Paul, of all people.

They drove through several villages, unspoiled and not unlike Stanton-le-Moor. The grey stone of the houses, the broad main street and village green were typical of the dales' villages.

It took them half-an-hour to reach Hatton Stacy and when they got there, Anna instantly became silent. In the first place, it was hard to find a place to park; there was no proper carpark and all visiting vehicles were parked alongside the Easter Beck for more than a mile from the village. Once they had found a space, they walked in silence along the road into the village.

When they finally reached the first of the houses, Anna was immediately aware of the charm of the cottages built around the beck. It was then that her quietness became grim and she dared not glance at her companion—she knew now why he had brought her here. On one side of the beck and surrounding the green were what had once been a pretty row of cottages.

Paul paused and looked in the window of each one and Anna had to stop by his side. She was counting them up one by one; Esterdale Woollens, then the post office and store, Ye

Olde Tea-Room, White Rose Crafts, then a break for the Farmers' Arms and coach-loads of tourists; after that was the Museum of Rural Life and a gift shop full of cheap pottery animals and fake horse brasses.

Around each establishment were crowds of people, making it almost impossible to walk on the pavement. Looking across the green, Anna could see people sitting by the beck with children shouting and splashing about in the water.

'It's a pretty village, isn't it, Anna?' Paul said in a dangerously smooth voice, and Anna didn't trust herself to reply. 'Would you like to visit the tea-room?'

'No, thank you, Paul.'

'We'll get back to the car then and drive farther up the dale. There's another village at the dale head—in fact, it's called Esterdale Head. It's not as big as Hatton Stacy, but very pretty.'

By the time they had reached the car and Anna had seen that even more cars were parked beyond them, she was seething with rage.

She climbed into the car and turned to Paul and for the life of her she could not stop herself hitting out at him as he put the key into the ignition.

'You did it deliberately! You brought me here to make me think it could happen to Stanton-le-Moor. You knew I would hate it.

And I hate you, too!'

Paul turned to her with a quiet smile. 'I can assure you, Anna, that I didn't mean to upset you so much. I thought you must be well-versed in these things and I can truthfully tell you that not so many years ago, Hatton Stacy was just like Stanton-le-Moor.'

'I don't believe it!' she cried out. 'Hatton Stacy is a honey-pot village, where everyone goes. What I plan to do in Stanton would only attract the passing motorist—it's not the same at all. You won't stop me. I'm not going to do anything to spoil the village—I wouldn't want to.'

While she was speaking, Paul had driven off up the dale and had taken a turning that rose steeply to the edge of the moor. He parked suddenly at the end of a broad track and looked at her.

'Honestly, Anna, I didn't mean to upset you. I'll try to make up for it now by taking you to one of my favourite places. As you can see, no cars come up here where it's necessary to walk for more than a few yards. Have you got sensible shoes on?'

She shot a glance at him, wondering whether he was serious.

'Yes, I have,' she answered.

'Right, off we go.'

Again they walked in silence, but this time the atmosphere between them was different. Up here, Anna felt she could forget the

63

irritations she had felt in Hatton Stacy. Besides, she had to concentrate on the steep and stony path. She was glad of the exercise because she could feel the stiff, upland breeze cutting out any warmth from the sun.

The track came to an end and Paul set off ahead of her, taking a path that was no more than sheep trod, winding its way through the newly-growing heather. By the time she had reached the top of the hill, Anna was out of breath and she was glad when Paul stopped. She caught up with him laughing. Then he put his arms round her from behind and gently turned her round. As her breath came more easily and she leaned back against him, she was aware not only of Paul's arms about her but of the fact that before them lay the whole of Esterdale. She was looking right down the valley, the green slopes steeply dipping to the trees clustered round the beck, villages and farms hidden in each fold of the hillside.

'Paul!' she exclaimed and there was gladness and excitement in her voice. 'You can see the whole dale from here—isn't it beautiful?'

'Yes, Anna,' he said. 'It is very beautiful—I thought you'd like it. Can you pick out Hatton Stacy now?'

'Yes, just a few buildings at the foot of that hill. How different it looks.'

'Yes, it does. Even people's feelings are different up here, Anna. Can you sense it? You're not angry with me any more, are you?'

He turned her gently in his arms so that she was facing him and she looked up into his eyes. They were soft grey pools of gentleness and she could hardly believe that she was looking at the same Paul Buxton she had come to resent and dislike.

He bent forward and touched her forehead with his lips and involuntarily she raised her head and offered her lips to his.

'No, Anna,' he murmured.

But then he was kissing her, a long, persistent but gentle kiss that seemed to hold some hidden meaning. Anna felt no strong or violent passion, but that same urgent wish arose in her as it had done on the occasion in the snow—that she did not want the kiss to end.

Paul lifted his head at last. 'You play the devil with my feelings, you little minx,' he said to her, and she was glad to hear the joking tone—it dispelled the emotion that was gathering between them. 'I didn't mean to kiss you before and I told you to forget it, didn't I? And now it's happened again.'

'Because of Marcia?' she asked rather rashly.

But he took it in good part. 'Yes, partly because of Marcia—which reminds me, we'd better get back and see if she's any better. Are you glad you came, Anna?'

'Yes, I am glad and I'm sorry I was cross— you've given me something to think about, but

65

I still want to open the tea-room.'

She took one last look down the dale, seeing only the beauty of the trees in their first leaf gathered round the Ester Beck as it wound slowly down the dale; and higher up, the hill farms, each with its solid, stone farmhouse permanent amongst the chequered fields and stone walls. And highest of all, the slopes of the moor where the sheep roamed amidst stretches of green hill pasture that gave way finally to the heather and the bracken. The whole dale was a paradox in the way it was delicately carved, but with a sense of strong and eternal ruggedness which human hand could not destroy.

Anna was thoughtful as they walked back to the car; she felt almost as though she was two people—the girl who loved the unspoiled, upper stretches of the dale and would gladly have them to herself, and the young person with a living to make who could see the justification for her tea-room in the village.

Paul was silent, too, and she was left wondering if it was not possible to reconcile the two conflicting feelings.

CHAPTER FIVE

That evening, her quandary was in no way helped by the arrival of another anonymous letter. It had the same writing on the envelope and she felt like burning it without reading it. But with trembling fingers, she opened it, compelled to read its message.

It is no use trying to get round the hotel owner. He won't help you with your scheme. He is on our side.

As she sat looking at it, Anna realised that the notes were coming from someone who was watching her movements closely. She wondered if it was from one of the older residents who lived across the green—they would have the advantage of being able to watch her every movement.

Anna worried about the letter all the next day, and when the third one came the following night and she read its tense message, she knew she would have to tell someone. This letter had only two words.

GET OUT!

That afternoon, she walked up to the stables. Easter was over now, so perhaps Gerry wouldn't be too busy to speak to her. But to her great disappointment, he was out with the horses. She left a message asking him to give her a ring, adding impulsively that it was urgent and went home again.

One of her main problems, she realised, was that she had little to do; the decorating was finished, she had made a comfortable living-room for herself out of the small room next to the kitchen, and the two front rooms were standing white, clean and empty. She could do nothing until she had heard from the planning people, but she had not even been given a date telling her when her application would be considered.

Instead of phoning, Gerry came round to see her. It was early evening and he had changed out of his riding clothes and looked relaxed and good-looking in dark cords and a thick sweater.

He walked into one of her empty rooms, then turned and took her hands.

'You're worrying about something. It's not just the message that you left—I can see it in your face.'

She nodded and gave him the letters, watching as his face creased with a heavy frown as he read the words.

'I burned the first one,' she told him.

He looked at her. 'I'm sorry, Anna—this is not nice. Anonymous letters never are. Are you going to do anything about it?'

She glanced up, surprised. 'What can I do?'

'You could go to the police,' he suggested.

'Oh, no,' she burst out. 'I don't want to do that. I can't believe that anyone means me any real harm. But it's making me think, Gerry— perhaps I'm wrong about the tea-room.'

He put a hand on her shoulders and made her look up at him, 'Do you still want a tea-room at Gable End, Anna?'

She nodded. 'Yes, I do. I don't want to give

up the idea. I can't believe that one tea-room would spoil Stanton-le-Moor, or make it into a tourist attraction like Hatton Stacy. Paul Buxton took me over to see it, you know.'

Gerry's eyes searched hers. 'Did he indeed? That was crafty of him. But if that didn't make you change your mind, why should a few pathetic letters, pushed through the door by some crank, make you have second thoughts? Ignore them, Anna, is my advice. Don't let them worry you—go ahead with your plans. If I got permission, then I can't see why you shouldn't.'

Suddenly, Anna found herself flinging her arms around his neck, and laughing, he pulled her into a bear-like hug.

'Oh, Gerry, you are nice. You've really cheered me up. I could kiss you.'

'I don't mind,' he said, and their lips met in a brief and playful kiss which Anna pulled away from.

'Oh, I'm sorry, Gerry. I don't know what's got into me. It must be all this worry,' she said.

'And there was I thinking you were kissing me because you really wanted to,' he teased her. 'Come on, put on a jacket or something, and I'll take you out for a drink. Then tomorrow night we'll have that dinner I promised you.'

Gerry did his best to keep her mind from her worries that evening and succeeded. She enjoyed his cheerful company and his amusing stories about some of his novice riders. She decided to take his advice and forget the letters and even said that she would think about going to the stables and having riding lessons to help to pass the time.

But a week later, the letters were still coming, one each evening and Anna became more and more worried. She tried watching out for someone crossing the green, but the envelopes always seemed to drop through the letter-box at the very moment when she was off her guard and she saw nothing suspicious.

On the day that Anna found a letter on her doormat when she came down in the morning, she felt she couldn't stand it any longer. She always opened them even though Gerry had told her to burn them straight away; but there was a compulsion about them, even though she always regretted it when she read the words. The letters were always in the same vein, some were threats, all were unpleasant. This particular one was a long one and must have taken a long time to compose.

Have you withdrawn your application yet?

Do it quickly or you might regret it. We don't want you here.

Anna stamped her foot and started to cry. 'I'm not staying in today,' she said to herself. 'I'll go for a long walk and try to decide what to do. I can't stand it any longer. I'll have to do something—but why should I give in?'

Hastily, she found her walking boots,

packed up a lunch and set off carrying her rucksack. There was a long walk she had always planned to do—she had the map with her and thought she could find the way.

The climb out of the village on to the moor was steep but Anna was glad of the exertion. She was hot when she got to the top so she tied her sweater round her waist and had a drink. She sat for a long time looking at the view, beautiful in the spring sunshine, but for once, she saw nothing. Her thoughts were still back in the village. Who was it that hated her so much? She would have preferred a public meeting in the village hall to this undermining, secretive campaign.

She jumped up, suddenly determined to walk and walk until it was all far from her mind.

She was on the ridge road that ran the length of the dale and she strode out, finding it easy walking. She ate her sandwiches, looked at the map and decided to find a different route back to Stanton-le-Moor. A good, wide, green road which seemed to be running in the right direction tempted her, but as she realised that her steps were taking her downwards, she knew she must be descending into the next dale. She was not alarmed, though. All she had to do was continue on this good path until she reached the road, and then make her way back to Stanton-le-Moor along the lanes.

An hour passed and Anna began to feel

tired and worried—the path had not dipped down to the road as she had expected it to do. There was no sign of any village or habitation and she had an uneasy feeling that she was going in the wrong direction. The sun had disappeared behind a layer of grey cloud which threatened rain, so it was not easy to work out which way she was going. She had no compass and knew she'd been a fool for she knew that one of the first rules of walking over the moors was to carry a compass.

She kept going until she felt so weary she stopped for a rest and to drink the last of her water. She had finished her food, but that did not worry her—yet. Lifting her head and looking through the trees, she thought she spotted something that made her sit up quickly and become instantly alert. Some of the trees were in full leaf, showing their first sprays of bright, summer green, but others were still almost bare, and through the branches, she thought she had caught a glimpse of a church tower. Anna looked carefully. She could see no houses or cottages; perhaps the church was set above the village, she thought, and the houses were in the hollow below.

With renewed hope and energy, she stuck to the path and in a short space of time, she was passing the first of the houses. At the entrance to the village, a round millstone declared its name, Brompton-in-Fenbydale. As in Stanton, there was a small store-cum-post-office and

Anna made her way towards it. She bought herself a fruit drink and a bar of chocolate and at the same time, asked how far it was to Stanton-le-Moor.

'Over the top, fifteen miles—round the dale end, it's twenty miles,' came the reply from the postmistress.

Anna walked out of the shop in a daze. She looked at her watch—four o'clock. She had taken a whole day to walk fifteen miles over the top. It would be an impossibility to go back the same way even if she had the energy. And twenty miles by road! She gave a groan—all the time she thought she'd been walking back to Stanton, she had in fact been steadily moving farther away.

There was a seat on the small green and she sat down to eat her chocolate and to have her drink. What a fool she'd been, and now what was she to do? She wondered if Gerry would come and fetch her. She looked around for a telephone box and spotted one underneath a tree near what looked like a small chapel in the corner of the village green.

Three times Anna tried ringing the stables, but there was no reply. She was not really surprised.

In desperation, she tried Windhayes. Thankfully, Anna heard Linda reply and she told her tale of woe. Yes, Linda said, of course she would come, but would Anna mind waiting half-an-hour while she got cleared up.

Anna returned to the seat in thankfulness but feeling foolish. She was glad just to sit quietly to regain her strength and to gather her thoughts together.

When she saw a dark-green Jaguar car driving towards her, a long time before she had expected to see anyone, she could not believe her eyes.

It must be Paul. Whatever was he doing here?

He had obviously spotted her on the seat, as he stopped the car on the edge of the green and came walking in her direction. She could not tell from his expression what kind of mood he was in and waited for words of exasperation and impatience. She certainly did not expect kindness.

'Anne, my dear, whatever have you been doing?'

It was too much for Anna's tired and fretful state. She looked at his face, saw the soft expression in the grey eyes, rushed into his arms and burst into tears.

Paul held her close and let her cry, his hand stroking her head gently as he murmured her name. As she felt the comfort of his arms, Anna felt the fit of sobbing pass and at last she was able to raise her head and speak to him.

'I'm sorry, Paul, I didn't mean to cry. I was so pleased to see you. Why have you come? I phoned Linda. I am sorry,' she repeated.

As he smiled down at her, he took out a

handkerchief and wiped her eyes and then her cheeks, then Anna felt the wonderful softness of his lips on her wet face and she let him lead her to the seat where he sat with his arm about her.

'Better now?' he asked. 'I was standing at the desk when your call came through. Linda was very busy so I said I'd come and fetch you. Do you mind?'

She smiled warmly and shook her head. 'No, it's very kind of you. I'm afraid I've been very stupid today.'

'Tell me,' he said, looking down at her and taking her hands in his and holding them tight.

Anna glanced up at him and wondered how much to tell him. She was never quite sure which Paul she was going to encounter, but he seemed to be in a genial mood for the moment.

'To tell you the truth—' Anna started by speaking rather hesitantly, but then words came in a rush of confidence. 'You see, I was very worried and fed up and I just wanted to get out in the open for a day. But I mistook the path over the ridge and when I thought I was walking back to Stanton, I was in fact going in the opposite direction and ended up in Brompton-in-Fenbydale. It's no good being cross with me because I didn't have a compass—I know very well I should have had one but I forgot all about it. I usually keep one in my rucksack but it wasn't there—'

Paul interrupted her quietly. 'And what was it that was worrying you so much that you had to get away?'

She could only tell the truth. 'I've been getting anonymous letters, Paul, for over a week.'

'Anonymous letters?' he echoed with a frown. 'Do you mean threatening letters?'

'Yes, I do.' And then Anna found herself able to speak, to tell him about the letters and their contents. 'It's horrible, Paul—really frightening, at times.'

As she finished, he took her hands again and she liked the feeling of strength and confidence in them. But he didn't say anything and she looked into his face trying to imagine from his serious expression what his reaction was going to be.

His question, when it came, was so quiet and calm that it seemed to increase the shock it gave her.

'When are you going to give up, Anna?' he asked her.

Her eyes flew to his and she snatched her hands away.

'Oh, you, you—' She was at a loss for words. 'You sit there, quiet and kind and protective and make me think you're sympathetic, and all the time you're against me. I might have known what you'd really be thinking. I was a fool to tell you about the letters—I somehow imagined you'd want to help me.'

'Anna, I do want to help you.' His voice sounded urgent. 'Listen to me. I know I didn't like the idea in the first place—I made no secret of the fact. If the people of Stanton-le-Moor had been behind you, I would have forgotten my prejudice, I promise you. But it's not like that, is it? These damned letters prove that the whole village is against you. They may be nasty but they are trying to tell you something and you should listen.'

But Anna was in no mood to listen to reason. She was tired and tearful and angry with Paul Buxton.

'You wouldn't have forgotten your prejudice,' she shouted at him. 'You would have done all you could to stop me—I wouldn't even put it past you to write the letters yourself to try and scare me off.'

'Anna!'

She looked at him and knew she had gone too far.

'I'm sorry, Paul,' she muttered, 'I don't really think you would do a thing like that, but who can it be? Do you think I should go to the police?'

He shook his head. 'No, don't do that. It'll cause a lot of unpleasantness. I've been thinking since you told me about the letters and I've one or two suspicions of my own. Would you be willing to leave it to me, and can I see the letters?'

'Yes, if you want to—but you won't make

77

me change my mind. If I get the planning permission I shall go ahead.'

Anna knew that she was sounding petulant and childish but she didn't care. She watched Paul get to his feet and put out a hand to her.

'We won't talk about it any more,' he said. 'I believe you to be mistaken, and you resent my interference. I'm sorry about that, Anna. I'd like to have known you better.' He looked at her as though he was about to say more but then changed his mind. 'Come on—we must get back,' he added.

Anna got into the car thankfully and before they had driven more than a mile, she had fallen asleep. She woke up as Paul came to a stop, on the green in front of Gable End, and she smiled dreamily as he leaned over and kissed her cheek.

'Wake up, Sleeping Beauty.' He laughed. 'You've slept all the way home.'

'Thank you for coming to fetch me Paul,' she said. 'I'm sorry we always seem to disagree.'

'Not always, Anna,' he said. 'And I want you to promise that you'll come to me if you are worried—about anything.'

She remembered their moments of happy companionship, she remembered the closeness and the kisses. She, too, would like to know him better.

'Not always, Paul,' she repeated, 'and thank you for your offer.' She got out of the car and hurried into the house.

A hot bath helped to take a lot of her aches and tiredness away, but by the time she had cooked a meal and washed up and settled in front of the fire, Anna was beginning to feel sleepy again.

So when the loud knocking came at the front door, she was startled and immediately nervous. She almost didn't open the door, but the knocking came again and sounded urgent. It came as another shock as she opened the door to and it was Marcia Camberley standing outside.

'There you are,' her haughty neighbour said, without preamble. 'I want to see you. I want to know just what is going on between you and Paul Buxton!'

CHAPTER SIX

As Anna opened the front door wider, she found herself stammering. 'Come in, er— please come in, Mrs Camberley.'

She led her visitor through to her small living-room.

'This is where I'm living at the moment. If I can go ahead with my plans, I shall make a living-room upstairs.'

Marcia Camberley grunted as she sat down in the chair offered on one side of the fireplace. 'Never mind about your plans now. I'll speak to you about that later. It's Paul I want to talk about.'

Anna looked at the other woman in bewilderment.

As always, she was immaculately dressed and succeeded in making Anna feel, shabby in her worn jeans and sweater. But it was the accusation that mattered now—just what did the woman mean?

'I'm sorry, Mrs Camberley—'

'Oh, for goodness' sake, call me Marcia, I'm not that much older than you.' The interruption was impatient and waspish.

'Marcia, I'm afraid I don't know what you mean about Paul Buxton. I hardly know him.'

'You know him well enough to be taken over to Hatton Stacey on Easter Monday, and I've just seen you drive up with him—and I saw him kiss you.'

Marcia was glaring at her. Her eyes looked almost wild with outrage, Anna thought. What can it mean? I'd better try to stay calm.

'Paul took me to Hatton Stacey to show me what kind of village it was. If you must know, we quarrelled. He's trying to persuade me to give up my idea of the tea-room.'

'And today?'

Anna tried to keep calm. 'I'm afraid it was my fault today. I walked up the dale and got myself lost and ended up in Fenbydale. I phoned Linda at the hotel to ask if she would come and fetch me but she was busy so Paul came instead. That's all there was to it. I was very grateful to him.'

'And the kiss?'

Anna suddenly lost her calm. 'What is this? An inquisition? And what has it to do with you, Mrs Camberley?'

The good-looking face in front of her took on a set and unattractive expression. 'If you must know, Miss Anna Hadlee, Paul and I are hoping to be married in the not-too-distant future.'

Anna looked at her askance. She could hardly believe the words she had just heard. Paul and Marcia Camberley? Married? No, she could not believe it possible. Not the Paul she was getting to know in spite of the arguments, not the Paul who had taken her up the dale to look at the view, who had shown to her a side to his nature which she knew she could like very much. Paul and Marcia? Never!

'You look surprised.'

Anna was brought back to earth by the hard voice.

'I'm sorry, I had no idea. I'm pleased for you, Mrs Camberley.' Anna hardly knew what she was saying.

Marcia continued briskly, 'I wanted you to know how things stood, so that you wouldn't get ideas into your head. I understand you're very friendly with Gerry Pearson. I should stick to him if I were you and forget about Paul.'

Anna found herself listening to the voice but all the time thinking of Paul; she had the sudden memory of him saying after their first kiss, 'I didn't mean that to happen.'

Was Marcia telling the truth? She had no reason to disbelieve her—only a gut feeling.

'. . . and about this crazy idea of yours.' The words brought Anna back to the present with a jolt.

Marcia was leaning forward. 'I've not spoken to you about it before, but I want you to know that I am totally opposed to your plan. I agree with Paul's views about the village entirely.'

Anna was taken aback at the sudden onslaught, though something told her not to be surprised.

'I'm afraid Paul and I have disagreed several times over the subject of the tea-room,' she said stiffly. 'I realise, of course, that it would be next door to you, Mrs Camberley—'

'That is no problem if Paul and I are to be married.'

Anna chose to ignore the interruption. '—but the tea-room will be very small and I won't have loud music playing or anything like that.'

Her visitor stiffened. 'If I may say so, you seem to have missed the whole point of our objections—it will mean more cars parked on the green, dogs and children running around the village and that is not the worst thing. If you succeed in getting planning permission, there is no knowing what other ventures might be started up. The whole character of Stanton-le-Moor will be changed.'

Marcia Camberley's voice was getting shrill. 'I am not the only one who is opposed to it, you know; you might find there is a petition against it and I should be glad to sign it. We can't have young nobodies coming in from the cities and changing our quiet way of life.' At this point, she got up and started to walk out of the room. 'I have said what I came to say and I don't think I need to repeat my warning about Paul. Good-night.'

Anna breathed a sigh of relief as she shut the door behind the almost hysterical woman. She seemed to be very nervy and tense, Anna thought. Surely it couldn't be true about Paul? She hardly seemed his type at all.

Before she had time to think any more about it, there was another knock on the door.

Who on earth is it this time, she said to herself. I don't think I can stand any more today.

She opened the door to Gerry Pearson.

'Oh, Gerry,' she cried out, as he stepped into the hall, 'I'm go glad to see you.' And she threw herself into his arms.

He held her tight and his voice was cross and laughing at the same time.

'Hey, what's all this about, young Anna?' he said.

'I've just had another visitor,' she replied. 'I wonder you didn't fall over her. It was Marcia Camberley.'

'Marcia? What did she want?' Gerry asked.

'She told me to keep my hands off Paul Buxton. She had seen us together. And Gerry, she said they were going to be married. Is it true?'

'Phew,' he said, looking at her closely. 'That's the first I've heard of it, though Paul has known her for a long time, I believe. I wouldn't have thought she was his type at all; she's older for one thing and she keeps having these nervous breakdowns.'

'I thought she seemed rather uptight,' Anna said and told him of the conversation she had just had with Marcia.

'Are the letters still coming, Anna?' he asked her.

'Yes, there was one first thing this morning. They've always come in the evening before. It was the last straw—I went out all day and I got lost!'

He dropped a kiss on her forehead. 'You've had quite a day. Come on, I'll take you out. We needn't go far, just along to the White Hart at West Wykeham for a drink. Would you like to come, Anna?'

She made a face. 'I'm very tired really, but I think it would do me good and I would like to talk to you, Gerry.'

'Good girl. Off you go and get ready, then.'

Anna was thankful to pour her heart out to Gerry who was a kind and sympathetic listener. They sat by a blazing fire in the small bar of the White Hart and talked quietly and privately while a darts match was going on at the other end of the room. Gerry insisted on ordering food, saying that he had not eaten even if she had; they both had home-made steak pie and Anna enjoyed it.

Over coffee, Gerry asked her a sudden question. 'Are you thinking of giving up, Anna?'

She looked at him; how different from the way Paul had put the same question earlier that day.

'What do you think I should do, Gerry? I seem to have so many doubts. At one time, I was sure of what I wanted, but as each day goes by, my confidence seems to ebb away. I was so determined to fight, at one time, but those letters have really got me down. And now Marcia Camberley is talking about a petition, what chance have I got?'

Gerry reached out and took her hand. He gripped it tightly.

'Look at me, Anna, and tell me the truth. Is it really what you want to do? To run a tea-room and craft shop in Stanton, I mean.'

She met his eyes and could see that he was serious. 'Yes, I do want to do it, Gerry. It's not just awkwardness. I love it in Esterdale and I can't think of a nicer way of making a living for myself.'

He was still gripping her hands. 'In that case,' he said, 'go ahead. Don't let yourself be put off by a few people in the village. Look how they objected to the stables and now they're an accepted part of the scene and nothing has been spoiled. Forget the letters, Anna, forget Marcia and Paul and go ahead with your dream. If you don't get planning permission, the decision will be taken out of your hands, but in the meantime, keep fighting.'

Anna laughed aloud. 'Oh, Gerry, you are good for me—I'm so glad I came out tonight, I think I've been brooding about it too much.'

Gerry smiled back at her. 'Well, here's another suggestion. You said you were interested in learning to ride, so why not come down to the stables each day and come out with us? I'd like to have you along, Anna.'

'Shall I, Gerry?' There was a half-frown on her face.

'Yes. It'll do you good and what's more we'll get to know each other better and I should like that.'

Anna suddenly lost her worries and her hesitation. 'I'll do it—and while I'm away, they can drop as many letters as they like though my letter-box.' She stopped for a moment, thinking quietly. 'Isn't it strange, Gerry, that I've never been able to catch anyone bringing the letters? Except for this morning, they've always come after dark and I've never seen a soul.'

'I think it implies that it's someone very local, probably from across the green who sees what's going on,' he replied.

'Yes, I've thought the same. I don't suppose I shall ever find out if I'm not prepared to go to the police.' She looked into his friendly, kind eyes. 'It's been a lovely evening, Gerry, and I am grateful. But now I'm feeling tired, do you think you could take us home?'

Sitting in the Land-Rover outside Gable End, she said goodbye to him and thanked him again. His arm was along the back of the seat and his fingers gently pressed her shoulder. Anna looked up at him and he smiled at her; bending his head, he let his lips meet hers for a brief moment, and she was glad of the reassurance that the casual kiss did not turn to one of passion.

'I'll see you at the stables in the morning,' she said. 'Good-night, Gerry.'

* * *

During the next few weeks, Anna felt a happy change in her life. In the first place, the letters stopped coming. At first she could not believe it, but gradually she put the uneasy horror of them behind her and began to feel that they had been the work of some prankster who had soon tired of having to compose the letters so painstakingly from words cut out of a newspaper.

The other thing was her riding lessons with Gerry. Anna had never had anything to do with horses before, but she found that she not only had an aptitude for riding but a natural love for the animals. Often during the week, she was the only one to ride out at Gerry's side in the morning as the children came to him after school; at week-ends, she found that she was easily the eldest of his pupils but she didn't mind.

The stables were set in fields on the edge of Stanton Wood, and the wide track through the wood took them on to the open pasture on the lower slopes of the moor. The air was fresh and clear, primroses and celandine still nestled in the wood and the trees were bright with the green of spring and early summer.

Gerry was a pleasant companion and a good teacher. He was quite different in the saddle, quiet and serious whereas usually he was jovial and inclined to chat. Anna liked him, but had the uneasy feeling that he was getting to like her a little too much—certainly more than she would have wished.

In all that time, she saw nothing of Paul and heard from Linda that he was away making a tour of his other hotels; neither did she set eyes on her neighbour for which she was glad. She had no doubt that Marcia was keeping a careful eye on Gerry's Land-Rover which was often parked on the green, and she hoped that it would give the older woman the reassurance she seemed to need that Anna was not dallying with Paul.

Although Anna didn't see Paul, she often thought of him. They had disagreed many times, but she knew she had been attracted to him and had welcomed his kisses. She found it very hard to believe that he was going to marry Marcia.

She was even a little disturbed by the fact. She had no claim on Paul, but to imagine him with Marcia seemed far from being right. Sometimes she had a wild urge to see him, to ask him about it, even to quarrel with him—anything to be in his company again. Then, at these thoughts, she would tell herself not to be silly and how lucky she was to have Gerry in her life at that time.

The period of calm in her life was to end abruptly one fine day in early May. As she was getting ready for her riding lesson, she received a phone call from Gerry to say that she was the only one riding that morning and suggesting that she pack up some sandwiches. He would bring drinks and they would have a picnic lunch somewhere.

Anna was delighted and set off in jeans and a shirt, not even needing a jersey in the warm sunshine. They rode together for an hour. Anna sat easily in the saddle by now and enjoyed a canter when they reached the edge of the moor.

As she took her hat off and sat by Gerry's side to unpack the sandwiches, she felt more relaxed than she had done for a long time. She watched the horses grazing and feasted her eyes on the view back over Stanton-le-Moor, She ate hungrily and Gerry laughed at her, then produced some beakers and some cider. It was a merry lunch-time, then just as Anna was thinking how easy and uncomplicated Gerry was, she looked up to find his gaze fixed on her face.

'What is it, Gerry?' she asked, a little nervously.

'Anna, my darling, I can't wait any longer. I've been so patient all these weeks. Anna, I fell in love with you the moment I saw you. I've loved you more with every passing day. Will you marry me, Anna?'

He had taken her hand in his and she looked at him with shock and amazement in her eyes. She knew he liked her but he had never given her any clue that his feelings were running this deeply!

'But, Gerry—' she started to say.

'Oh, I know I'm much older than you are and that everyone thinks of me as a confirmed bachelor, but I know I could make you happy. I'm not asking for an answer now, Anna. I've given you a shock, haven't I? But, please, will you think about it? Say you will.'

Anna hardly knew how to reply and chose

her words carefully.

'Gerry, I'm very touched, but I'll have to be honest. I like you very much, but that's all. I can't pretend and I couldn't marry without love either. I'm very sorry, Gerry. I don't want to upset you or spoil our friendship, but I'm afraid the answer has to be no.'

He pulled her into his arms then and she felt his mouth seeking hers. The kiss lingered but suddenly and unbidden, Anna could see Paul's face, remember his words, though she did not know why she should think of him at such a time.

She drew away from Gerry guiltily and whispered, 'I'm sorry, Gerry.'

He hugged her in reply. 'I shan't give up hope. At least I know that you like me—that's enough for the time being. And now, shall we go home? I have to be back in time for my afternoon school crowd.'

They rode quietly back to the village and if Gerry was upset at Anna's refusal of his proposal of marriage, he didn't show it. She drove home from the stables and as she reached Gable End, she saw with a shock that Paul's Jaguar was parked next door. He must have got back, she thought, and felt a totally and unexpected lurch of the heart to know that he was near again. She tried to dismiss her emotional reaction and remind herself that it was Marcia he had come to see as soon as he returned.

CHAPTER SEVEN

That evening, she felt restless and uncertain after her conversation with Gerry. Also, in spite of his assurances and his encouragement, she also had moments of serious doubt about her wisdom at continuing with her plans. Sometimes, she felt she had been foolish to have thrown up a good job to come to this place; at others, she loved the house and the village so much that she made up her mind to remain patient and see if she was given a chance to put her plans into practice.

With thoughts chasing round in her head, she decided to have a walk up to the moor and to call in on Linda at Windhayes on the way back.

After having a quick chat with Linda and fixing up a meeting with her, Anna hurried out of the hotel and almost bumped into Paul who was on his way in.

'Anna, just the person I wanted to see,' he said, as his hands reached out to steady her.

She looked at him in some surprise. 'Did you get back today, Paul?'

'Yes, and I've been to see Marcia.' He was still holding her arm and he started to draw her towards the gate at the side of the hotel that led into the garden at the rear. 'Come and sit in the garden with me. There's something I want to ask you.'

He gave her no chance to reply and she followed him into the garden. The hotel was situated on the slope, rising to the moor and the garden at the back was rather unusual and beautiful. It had been designed in several terraces, each individual in character, with a gracious flight of steps leading to an enclosed garden.

Anna walked through the lowest terrace of shrubs, attractive for their foliage and then followed Paul up the first of the stone steps and found herself in a secluded garden which looked over the roof-tops of the village far below. He sat down on a wooden seat and obviously expected her to place herself beside him. She was feeling curious about his motives for bringing her here.

His first question was to the point and easy to answer. 'Have you had any more anonymous letters, Anna?'

She shook her head. 'No, they seem to have stopped, thank goodness. I haven't had any for a couple of weeks—perhaps that's the last of it.'

But his next question was to make her feel angry and she found she could hardly answer it with equanimity.

'And you haven't changed your mind in that time? I understand you've been seeing a lot of Gerry Pearson. No doubt he's encouraged you in your folly?'

93

'Paul Buxton, whatever has it to do with you whether I've been seeing Gerry or not? As it happens, I've been having riding lessons, but that hardly concerns you.' Her eyes sparked with anger, but when they met his, they encountered only a look of softness, not the angry irony she had been expecting.

'Anna, if only you knew,' he said enigmatically. 'I care enough about you to think that a friendship between you and Gerry Pearson is entirely wrong—he must be nearly twice your age in the first place.'

Anna jumped from the seat and confronted him. 'You can't say things like that—you know nothing about it! If you must know, Gerry has asked me to marry him!'

She felt her arms caught in a vice like grip. 'But you won't marry him, do you hear? That's the last thing I want to see.'

She was astonished.

'But, Paul, what has it to do with you? It's what I think that matters. You don't come into it at all—what right have you to make a fuss like this?' She was still staring at him, unable to understand half of what he was saying to her. 'In any case, how can you make objections to me seeing Gerry, if you're going to marry Marcia?'

'If I'm what?' The words came with the staccato sound of gunfire.

Anna hesitated. 'if you are going to— Marcia told me you were going to marry her.'

'Would you mind repeating that?' His voice was grim.

'Marcia told me that you were going to—that you were hoping to be married soon.'

Her words dropped into stony silence and she looked into a face rigid with pent-up anger.

'Did she now?' he said and before she realised what was happening, Paul had pulled Anna down towards him on the seat. She almost fell against him and found herself caught in a steel-like embrace while his mouth found her lips. His anger was in the kiss yet she felt he was asking her to return the hidden emotion. He gave a half-groan and became more gentle with her.

Anna felt a throbbing fire run through her and she couldn't stop herself from pressing closer to him. All thought had fled, and there was nothing left but the sensation—the sensation of Paul's closeness and his demands.

There was still anger in his voice when he eventually spoke but it was tempered by a strange gentleness. 'And now, Anna Hadlee, tell me if I can feel like that for you and be wanting to marry Marcia at the same time. What have you to say to that?'

Anna looked at him almost fearfully. 'I don't understand anything, Paul. All I know is that Marcia has suspicions about us, you and me, and came to warn me off. It was then she told me about you getting married.'

'Anna.' He was looking into her eyes and she would have called the expression there beseeching. 'Before I do anything else, before I say the things I wanted to say to you, I'm going to see Marcia Camberley. Come along. I'll give you a lift into the village.'

We almost ran back to the car and Anna followed him closely. Not a word was said during the short ride into the village and outside Gable End, Paul turned to her.

'I shall be away all tomorrow, but I shall hope to see you the following day, and I might have something to ask you.'

His tone was still aggressive and he pulled her against him and kissed her quickly before releasing her so that she could get out of the car.

For the rest of that evening, Anna was bewildered. A proposal from Gerry and such odd behaviour from Paul, all in one day, was too much. But one thing was made very clear to her—as long as Paul Buxton had the power to sway her emotions and her senses the way he had done that night, she knew she would never be able to marry Gerry Pearson.

Next morning, she came downstairs to an anonymous letter. She could not believe it.

You thought you had got away with it, but you have gone too far. Beware danger.

The tone of the letter was so different and so vindictive that Anna felt frightened. Gerry laughed if off later that morning and she felt unusually at odds with him. She met Linda in the evening who was convinced that she should go to the police.

It was dark when she got home from their evening out and as she put her key into the front door lock, she had a prickling sense of fright and fear and didn't know which of her senses had been alerted. There was a strange smell, an ominous crackling sound, and when she grasped the door knob, it felt hot. She opened the door and a scream stopped in her throat—flames leaped out at her and the heat forced her back.

*   *   *

Anna's immediate instinct was to slam the front door shut and to run as fast as she could to Marcia Camberley next door.

'Marcia,' she managed to gasp as the door opened and she pushed past the woman standing there. 'Fire—phone—'

She caught sight of the phone on the hall table and without waiting for Marcia to reply, she quickly dialled 999. Breathless, she gave the details and only then did she turn back to Marcia who was still standing strangely immobile.

'I opened the front door, Marcia—it's all ablaze. What shall I do?'

'You can do nothing till the fire engine comes.'

Anna looked at the older woman blankly. She had expected hysterics, but there was only this strange, rigid calm about her.

'Hadn't we better go outside, Marcia? It could spread to your house—' She was panicking in all she was saying and started for the front door.

'The walls between these houses are at least three feet thick. Don't worry.'

Anna looked at Marcia Camberley. Perhaps she's in shock, she thought. Should I do something? Her own fear took over. She rushed outside again to find herself confronted by a group of shouting and jostling people. One look at her door told her what had brought them—the flames had eaten through the wood and were blazing round the thick door posts.

'Oh,' she cried out loud urging the fire engine to come. 'Hurry up, hurry up, my house.' Tears were streaming down her face but no-one approached her or said anything to her. There was an eerie sense of suspicion and alarm amidst the small crowd. As Anna looked for a friendly face, there was a screech of brakes and a Land-Rover pulled up. Gerry jumped out and ran towards her.

'Oh, Gerry,' Anna sobbed, glad to run into his arms and to be held tightly and securely.

'Anna, are you all right?' he said roughly.

'Yes, I'm all right, but the house—how could it have happened?' She broke off as

98

another car drove up and in seconds, Paul was running towards the house. He stopped short as he saw Anna in Gerry's arms.

'Anna, I heard that—oh, but I see that you are all right with Mr Pearson.'

Anna hardly recognised him, the edge to his voice was so strained. She stepped towards him and put out a hand, but he ignored it.

'How did you know about it, Paul?'

'Marcia phoned me,' he said abruptly. 'Is the fire engine on its way? How did it happen?'

His question was never answered as the wailing siren of the fire engine was heard from the bridge and seconds later, all was action and alarm. Hoses were joined to the hydrant in an instant and played on to the house. The front door disintegrated and a gasp went up from the crowd as the inferno inside was seen. Anna shut her eyes in horror, then opened them again to look for Paul. She caught sight of him disappearing into Marcia's cottage and as she turned, she found herself once again enfolded in Gerry's arms. She was glad to hang on to him, but could hardly answer his questions.

'Do you know how it started, Anna?'

She shook her head. 'I just came home, opened the door and found it ablaze. I'd been out with Linda. Oh, Gerry, do you think I'm going to lose all the house? I can't understand what could have started it—the wiring was new and so was the central heating. It wasn't on in any case.'

'You didn't leave a fire on?' he asked.

'No. it's been so mild, I haven't needed fires,' she replied.

Gerry's hand tightened on her arm and he nodded towards the crowd. 'I think the chief fire officer is looking for you, Anna.'

'I understand it's your house, miss,' a uniformed officer said as he came up to her. 'Try not to worry too much. As far as we can see up to now, it's just the stairs that are alight. The doors into the other rooms were shut, fortunately, so that's contained it. We'll soon have it under control.'

An hour later, Anna was allowed in and saw that the staircase had collapsed completely, but the fireman assured her that there was no damage upstairs except from the water. The downstairs rooms with their sturdy, old doors were untouched, though the doors themselves were charred and black.

Anna felt sick and shaky. At the back of her mind, she was remembering the words of the letter she had received that morning. 'Beware danger' it had said. Had the fire been started deliberately? Who could possibly have done such a thing? She felt too confused and frightened to voice her worries—even to Gerry, who was still by her side.

As she came out on to the green again, she saw that people were beginning to drift away and Paul was standing talking to the fire officer.

He turned towards her. 'Anna, everything's safe now, but they're going to leave a man here all night as a precaution. In the morning, the forensic team will move in and I expect the police will want to see you.' He looked at her searchingly, then at Gerry, and back to her again. 'Anna, I think you'd better come back to the hotel with me. Don't you think that's the best thing for her, Pearson?' He raised his eyebrows questioningly in the other man's direction.

Gerry nodded and seemed glad. 'I'd be very grateful, I can hardly ask her to my place.' He kissed Anna's cheek. 'I'll see you in the morning. Take care.'

Anna watched him striding towards the Land-Rover and, even in her weariness, was aware of the proprietorial air which he had used towards her. What must Paul think?

But Paul was guiding her towards the Jaguar and she stumbled along, hardly knowing what she was doing.

At Windhayes, she let him take her into the kitchen and make her strong coffee, laced with brandy and she sipped it thankfully.

'What are you thinking about, Anna?' he said quietly.

'Oh, Paul.' And suddenly she began sobbing and his arms came about her. He was murmuring her name over and over.

'Paul, I must tell someone. There was a letter this morning. It was different from the others—more threatening.' And she told him what it had said.

'So you're wondering if the fire was started deliberately?'

'Yes.'

'I don't know what to say to you, Anna.' He sighed. 'It's a possibility but we'll have to wait and see what the investigations reveal. The forensic men will be here first thing in the morning and they'll soon find the cause of the fire.'

'Will they?'

'Yes, they are experts, after all.' He smiled teasingly at her. 'They know exactly what to look for. What I want you to do is to go and have a bath while I sort out a room for you. I'll go and find Michael and we'll see if someone can lend you some nightclothes. Stay here and drink your coffee, I won't be long.'

Michael came in minutes later, very concerned about her and soon had things arranged.

Then she went to the front of the hotel to say goodbye to Paul, her stomach churning a little. She had the feeling that he was still disturbed by the attentions of Gerry and wished she could dispel his worried look and part from him on good terms. For once, it seemed, her wish was to be granted.

Standing on the front steps, he took both

her hands in his and his touch was gentle, his look concerned.

'I know it's easy for me to say it, but try not to worry, Anna. We'll try to sort out the mystery and I'll help you all I can to get the house to rights again. And, believe me—I may have opposed you in the past, but I wouldn't for the world have had this happen to you. Look at me, Anna.'

In the light of the outside lantern, Anna looked up into his eyes and the expression made her catch her breath.

'Paul,' she said softly, 'you are very kind.'

She was drawn within the circle of his arms and his lips touched hers briefly. 'Good-night, Anna. I wish I could do more for you. Try to get a good night's sleep and I'll come and see you in the morning.'

She reached up and kissed him again—it seemed a very natural gesture. 'Good-night, Paul, and thank you.'

She watched as he ran down the steps and drove off in his car, then turning with an odd and comforting mixture of tiredness and happiness, she went back into the hotel. She had a welcome bath and found herself in the same bedroom she had occupied before. She was glad of this, as it was familiar and secure. She was certain she would not sleep, but fell into bed exhausted and snatched a few hours.

CHAPTER EIGHT

It was in the early hours of daylight that Anna awoke with a start and her mind went over the events of the previous evening again. Although she had harboured many doubts about the tea-room, she had never dreamed that anyone could be so opposed to it that they would set fire to the house. It was this thought that worried her more than any other and would not go away.

Anna got up early, dressed and had a walk in the garden before breakfast. The fresh, morning air cleared her mind and she was amazed to find that she felt hungry. When she went back into the hotel, it was to find that both Paul and Linda had arrived. Linda was horrified at the news; she lived on the outskirts of the village and had not heard about the fire until now.

Paul wore an anxious smile and there was concern in his eyes, which changed to relief when he realised she was composed and self-possessed.

'Have breakfast with me, Anna,' he said. 'I didn't have any at home and I thought I'd have to persuade you to eat.'

She smiled briefly. 'No, I'm quite hungry, and there's a lot to be done today so it's only sensible to have a decent breakfast.'

'Good girl,' he said.

Anna was glad of Paul's presence that morning; he was both helpful and practical and was able to remind her of all the things that had to be done.

The police and the fire-officer arrived soon after nine and it was a long interview. Together they went down to Gable End where Anna nearly wept when she saw the charred remains of her lovely wooden staircase. The forensic men were busy, but Anna was able to see at a glance what would need to be done. Paul took her through to the back door by way of Marcia's garden, but Marcia had very little to say. She tried to catch Paul's arm but he would not stop and Anna could sense the resentment against herself for claiming Paul's attention.

Anna found, to her relief, that her kitchen and living-room were untouched and she was able to find all the documents she needed for insurance purposes. Back at the hotel, Paul insisted that she contact her insurance company straight away and she also had a word with the same builder who had done all the work on her house just a few short months ago.

Gerry turned up in the middle of the morning and they all had coffee together, but the atmosphere between the two men was strained and it upset Anna, knowing she was the cause of it.

After Gerry had gone, Anna looked at Paul and she could see a frown between his eyes. For some reason she could tell he disapproved of Gerry and she found it hard to understand; it almost seemed like jealousy but she told herself that this was ridiculous—he hadn't placed any claim on her and indeed, seemed glad to be rid of her on most occasions.

Over lunch, she and Paul almost came to blows once again and Anna was sorry as she was really ready to appreciate all he was doing for her.

'You'll stay here while the house is being put right, of course,' he suddenly said to her.

Anna was dismayed. She remembered how much it had cost her for her previous stay and she really didn't think that she was in the position to be able to afford that kind of expense.

'Thank you, Paul,' she said, 'but I'm afraid I shall have to took for a room somewhere in the village. You see, the hotel is a little beyond my reach—and with all the expense of the house, even if the insurance does cover most of it, I shall have to be careful.'

He looked straight at her, offended. 'Anna, I'm asking you to stay as my guest—I wouldn't dream of charging you in the circumstances.'

She was touched. 'But, Paul,' she protested, 'it could be weeks before Gable End is ready. It's very kind of you to offer but I'll have to refuse.'

'You won't have to refuse,' he said stubbornly. 'That room you were in last night is yours for as long as you need it, and I won't take a penny.'

'I can't, Paul, I can't,' she insisted, just as stubbornly. 'I must contribute something.'

'Anna Hadlee!' He was almost shouting at her. 'I want you under this roof where you're safe. If your conscience is worrying you about the cost, then give Linda a hand or something—help out in the kitchens if you like. They'll soon be needing extra help in anyway as the season gets started.'

Was he serious? I'll take him at his word, Anna thought. She smiled.

'But, Paul, I'd be delighted to do something in the hotel—I don't mind what it is. The time will hang very heavily for me if I have nothing to do. Do you really mean it?'

He grinned suddenly and she thought how young and handsome he could look. 'You're an impossible girl—I didn't really mean it, but if it'll make you any happier and will keep you occupied then I'll speak to Michael. And you will stay in that room on the third floor—is that settled?'

Anna put out a hand and he seemed glad to take it and hold on to it; as always, his touch sent a thrill through her and she smiled at him again.

'Thank you very much, Paul, I'd be most grateful and it'll see me through a difficult

107

period, though I've always got Gerry, of course.' The moment the words were out she regretted them.

Paul dropped her hand and his face went blank. 'So I'd noticed,' he said and he got up and walked away from the table, leaving Anna with tears pricking at her eyes at his sudden change in mood.

He acts as though he's jealous of Gerry, she thought, but that just doesn't make sense. He has Marcia and I mean nothing to him—I can't do, otherwise he wouldn't still be seeing her. Sometimes I wish I'd met him under more normal circumstances, but—oh, what's the use?

That, however, was not to be the end of her troubles that day. Just as Paul was preparing to leave Windhayes to go into Leeds that afternoon, the fire officer from the night before arrived together with a man in a plain grey suit.

'Miss Hadlee, we need to see you urgently. You can have Mr Buxton with you if you wish. This is Detective Inspector Maunder from Kirby Hayton.'

Anna felt nervous and mystified and she was glad that Paul was there and ready to speak.

'Won't you come into the office?' he said. 'Would you like tea?'

'Thank you.' The words were short and matter-of-fact and Paul sent a message to the kitchen.

They all sat round Michael's table and the fire officer was the first to speak. 'Miss Hadlee, we have received the initial report of the forensic team and there is no question that the fire in your house was started at the front door. We have no reason to doubt that a rag soaked in paraffin was pushed through the letterbox and ignited. We are dealing with a case of arson.'

Anna felt the blood drain from her face and the figures in front of her seemed blurred and faint. Then she felt Paul's hand on hers, gripping tightly and willing her to understand and face up to what she had just heard. Although Anna had received the warning the previous morning, she still found it hard to believe that what had been said was true— someone had set fire to her home.

She could not find her voice and then she heard Paul speaking. He was telling the officer about her plan for the tea-room and of the opposition in the village. He told them about the anonymous letters and in particular of the threatening letter she had received on the same morning of the fire.

The police inspector interrupted. 'Do you have any of those letters with you, Miss Hadlee, or did you destroy them?'

She spoke at last and her voice was hoarse and faint. 'They're upstairs. I brought them with me. I have been wondering, you see . . .'

'Perhaps you'd like to go and fetch them while Mr Buxton puts us in the picture.'

After that, it seemed like hours of questioning. Anna answered when she could and Paul helped her when she couldn't. He never once let it be known that he was one of the people opposed to the plan. He remained neutral throughout and she felt glad.

Paul insisted, at the end of it all, that he should take her to the house to fetch what she would need from her bedroom. The investigating firemen put up a ladder that reached to the top landing and Paul helped her up. Her bedroom was as usual except for the dreadful smell of burned timbers. But it broke her heart to remain in her poor, ruined house for long. She hurried to pack a case and handed it down to one of the men. They arranged for the front door to be boarded up after that and Paul took her back to Windhayes. He was anxious to be off to Leeds and she didn't want to delay him any longer. There was anxiety in his eyes as she stood by the car to see him off.

Anna saw his expression and managed a smile. 'Don't worry, Paul, I'll be all right, and thank you for all you have done.'

He put his hands on her shoulders and, bending his head, met her lips softly with his own.

'I wish I had the right to do more,' he said quietly, then, giving her a quick hug, got into his car and drove away.

She stood there motionless for many minutes; the touch of his lips and such remarks as he had just made seemed to tell her so many things, yet the situation was confused between them. There were times when she felt she would dearly love to be closer to Paul Buxton. She often felt a strong and somehow forbidden feeling that here was a man she could come to love. Then circumstances would change and a rift would open up between them again. Anna knew then that she must put her longings to the back of her mind. It was a hopeless situation all round and best forgotten.

Things moved quickly during those next weeks. The insurance company settled promptly and the builders took over in no time. Their first job after removing the burned timber was to fit a new front door and once that was done, Anna felt easier in her mind. She was kept busy at the hotel and Linda took advantage of having her there to take a few days off.

As time went by, Anna was amused and delighted to discover that Linda and Michael were on more than friendly terms and it gave her a lot of pleasure to feel that there might be a romance between them.

She was glad of the occupation that helping out at Windhayes gave her. It helped to offset the continual nagging worry that there was someone in the village out to do her harm.

She had many sessions with the police whose local enquiries had revealed no evidence of any value. It was their impression, they told her, that the criminal act had been committed by a person who had watched her movements closely, and at a time when that person knew she was out of the house and shortly to return. Therefore, they did not appear to want to harm her, merely to scare her by causing some damage to the house. She had come home in time to prevent the fire spreading and mercifully the damage was slight and she was unscathed.

The police seemed to be interested in the movements of all those who were aware of Anna's habits and comings and goings. Houses were searched, people were questioned but no information of any value was forthcoming.

Anna stopped the riding lessons, but continued to see Gerry in spite of a difference of opinion with him on the very night that Paul had left her at the hotel. She had been feeling very tired and did not know quite what to do with herself that evening. Her mind was in turmoil and when Gerry appeared, she was more than pleased to see him.

'Anna, you're looking tired,' he said as he greeted her. 'Do you feel like coming for a short walk? Fresh air and the exercise might do you good.'

She nodded gladly. 'Yes, I think it's just what I need, Gerry—and there's so much to tell you.'

They walked from the hotel on to the moor, but Anna was hardly aware of her surroundings. She told Gerry of the investigation's findings and he was alarmed.

'Anna, it's just not safe for you! Who could have done such a thing? You could have been trapped. What are you going to do?'

'I'm not going to be defeated by a madman, Gerry. I'll have the house repaired and move back in. Whether I proceed with my plans is another matter. I can't even think that far ahead at the moment. Fortunately, Paul is letting me stay at Windhayes in return for me acting as deputy receptionist, washer-upper, chamber-maid or whatever is available. No, don't look so disgusted. I told him that I would only stay there if he let me do something towards my keep, so we struck a bargain.'

But Gerry was slowing her down and made her stop and face him, putting his hands firmly on her shoulders. 'Anna, there's no need for that. There's a much easier and happier solution. Marry me straight away, Anna. Come to my place as my wife and you'll be safe for always. I'm serious, Anna.'

His voice was urgent and persuasive, but Anna was shaking her head.

'Oh, I'm sorry, Gerry, but I can't marry you for those reasons. You're so kind, but I'll only marry when I know I really love someone and you know how I feel about you. It just isn't enough.'

For once, Gerry seemed to lose his habitual good humour and spoke grudgingly. 'Yes, I think I do know how you feel. I've seen you looking at Paul Buxton. I think that's where your true feelings lie. Am I right?'

But Anna shook her head vehemently. 'No. Marcia told me she was going to marry him— and he didn't deny it.'

Even as she spoke, she remembered Paul's peculiar and violent reaction to her mention of Marcia's name, and she remembered also some of the imponderable things he had said to her since.

Gerry grunted. 'I'll believe that one when I see them together in church. Marcia has some strange ideas and she's well-known for behaving oddly.'

'She didn't have hysterics last night when I went in to phone,' Anna replied, and told Gerry how strange she had found Marcia's reaction.

'She probably set fire to Gable End herself,' he said unreasonably.

'Oh, Gerry, don't talk nonsense—she's a rational, adult woman, not a maniac.'

'I wouldn't be so sure about that,' he said grimly. 'But I refuse to talk about the woman—I want to talk about you. If I promise not to mention marriage again, will you still come out with me, Anna?'

She smiled at him. 'You're too good-natured, Gerry. I've just turned you down and you offer to be my friend. But I can't say no— I'd love to go on seeing you even if I can't have riding lessons while I'm working at Windhayes.'

After that, she saw Gerry regularly and Paul not at all. He was away on one of his trips visiting his hotels and she had no contact from him and was aware of a keen sense of disappointment.

She didn't see Marcia either, not even to pass the time of day, and she was glad. She was down at Gable End most days to see how the work was getting on but she did not call on Marcia after the very first day when she had gone in to thank her for letting her use the phone. She found her neighbour morose and moody as usual, so she didn't stay long, neither did she feel encouraged to call again. She guessed the ill-humour must be because Paul was away. What on earth did he see in such a woman, she wondered.

Although she put all thoughts of the tea-room to the back of her mind, each day she found herself expecting to hear the result of the planning inquiry. Almost two months had gone by since she had made the application. She realised that she must have missed one meeting of the planning committee and was waiting for the next.

At last the day came when Anna was ready to move back to Gable End. There was only a lingering smell of the fire and the builders had made a splendid job of the new staircase—she had decided to put in a dark wood staircase which suited the character of the old house. Redecoration was complete and she thankfully unpacked her case in the bedroom, glad to be home again.

She felt a slight sense of nervousness that night, but managed to sleep and when she went downstairs next morning to see a letter lying on the mat, her heart missed a beat. Surely the anonymous letters were not going to start again!

When she picked up the envelope and turned it over, she saw with some relief that it was an official, typewritten letter and she opened it quickly.

She could not believe her eyes when she picked out the main gist of the letter.

. . . for the conversion of Gable End in the village of Stanton-le-Moor, N. Yorks. We are pleased to inform you that your application has been successful . . .

CHAPTER NINE

Holding the letter in trembling fingers, Anna read the few lines over and over again.

She could have her tea-room—she had won! She could have it! She felt tears of joy streaming down her cheeks, but they gradually turned to sobs as she stumbled back into the living-room. She collapsed on to the settee, half-crying and half-laughing.

'I don't want a tea-room,' she cried out loud. 'I don't want it any more.'

And it was true. She had gained a victory, but it was a hollow victory, borne out of her own obstinacy. Anna realised then, as she thought and thought about it, that for a long time she had known that she didn't want Stanton-Le-Moor spoiled any more than its inhabitants did. Her own determination and stubbornness to have her way had been fuelled by Paul's opposition, and then, when the letters had started to arrive, by her anger and the feeling that nothing would stop her.

Several brief scenes and memories came to her mind; the village as she had always known it in Aunt Beattie's day; the trip to Hatton Stacey with Paul and the shocked upset she had received—even the scene outside Gable End when her house was burning had been significant. She had received no sympathy or support from anyone in the village and these things all told her now that her dream had been doomed from the start.

Paul had been right all along.

The acquisition of the house and the money that went with it had gone to her head, she thought, and she had not been prepared to listen to reason.

Well, that's the end of that, Anna was thinking. I'm not going to go ahead with it. The village will be pleased and so will Paul. She rather liked the idea that Paul might be pleased with her and suddenly felt an enormous sense of relief that somehow the decision seemed to have been made for her.

She was spurred into action. Within half an hour, she had replied in a carefully-worded letter to the planning authorities, decided to put the house on the market and rang up an estate agent in Kirby Hayton. Then she sat down to think.

If she got a good price for the house, she would have enough money to buy herself a small, terraced property somewhere in Leeds where she knew she would be able to get a job. Another of her dreams would be over and she would return to the city and forget about life in the dales. She would burn the letters, put the animosity behind her and—perhaps the hardest part—she would have to forget about Paul and Gerry. Gerry would be disappointed, but she didn't love him and he'd have to learn to accept it. And Paul had Marcia. She must forget Paul, put him out of her life once and for all.

The estate agent came that afternoon and by five o'clock there was a 'For Sale' sign at the front of Gable End. She had phoned Gerry to tell him what she was doing and had met with the expected protestations and a further proposal of marriage. However, Anna had made up her mind. She had also decided to leave the house empty and to lose no time in moving back to Leeds, for a job was becoming important.

At six o'clock, her evening meal was interrupted by a loud banging on the front door.

Anna opened the door to an angry Paul.

'I've just got back,' he shouted at her. 'What does it mean "For Sale"? What are you doing?'

'Come and sit down, Paul. I'll make you some coffee,' she said, pleased that at least she'd have the chance to say goodbye to him.

'I don't want coffee, I want explanations,' he raged. 'What on earth are you doing? What about the tea-room? Has your application been turned down and you're moving out in a fit of pique?'

Anna, too, was angry by this time but she managed to remain calm as she spoke to him. She told him about the planning application and her reaction to it. She confessed that she hadn't been happy in her mind since the fire— it had been caused to make her change her mind and it had succeeded. So she was selling the house and going back to Leeds to work.

Paul was quiet then and looked at her pensively. 'But, Anna, you love the village, you love the dale. I thought you didn't like city life?'

'I have no choice, Paul. I have a little money from Aunt Beattie, but I'm not well-off. I must earn a living. I plan to buy a small house in Leeds, somewhere in Headingley, perhaps, where I had the flat—it's nice there and not too far into the city.'

He got to his feet and held out his hands to her. Slowly, she put hers into them, wondering what his expression meant. Without saying anything, he pulled her into his arms, and tilted her face up to his so that she looked into his eyes. She had never seen them so clear and caring—what was he going to say to her?

But there were no words to be said.

She felt his mouth on hers, demanding a response and as she felt the length of his body strained against hers, she knew a desire that was not passion alone. Here was the man she had come to love. Was this to be her answer?

He pulled away.

'Anna, Anna, what am I doing? What can I say?'

She knew instantly that she was not going to hear words of love from him. There was still an obstacle between them. To hide her own shaken feelings, Anna spoke with a false cheerfulness, saying the first thing that came into her head.

'You don't have to say anything, Paul. I understand—you have Marcia to think of.'

'And you have Gerry,' he replied quietly. 'I saw you on the night of the fire.'

She didn't tell him that Gerry meant nothing in her life—that it was Paul himself who was about to break her heart.

'Yes, I have Gerry,' she said.

He turned from her brusquely. 'So I won't see you again, Anna. I'll say goodbye and wish you the best of luck. I almost wish that you could be here with your damned tea-room.'

With these mystifying words, he turned and left her, saying no more, but shutting the front door firmly behind him. Anna saw him get into the car and drive furiously away in the direction of the hotel.

He hasn't gone in to Marcia, she thought as she watched the car disappear up the hill. Oh, Paul, what could have been between us, her heart cried out. But she knew she must be sensible and occupy her mind with her move to Leeds.

Two days later, she had packed up, put what little furniture she had into store, left the key with the estate agent and was on her way out of Esterdale. She had had an emotional scene with Gerry the previous evening, but his pleadings did not reach her and all she could do was to promise to keep in touch with him.

In Leeds, she booked into a guest house and went flat hunting. It was not too difficult—student rooms were hard to come by, but she was looking for a bigger flat and there seemed to be plenty of these available. She settled on Headingley again, being the part she knew best and although the flat was smaller than her previous one, it had the advantage of being on the ground floor with access to a rather overgrown back garden which she thought she might like to tackle.

The right job was not so easy to come by, but she scanned the papers and went round the employment agencies. A week later, she was pleased to receive a phone call asking her to go for an interview at the television studios. It was a complete change and a new challenge to her. She hadn't even held out much hope of getting an interview because of her lack of experience, so when they offered her the job she was delighted, and accepted it right away.

During the first months back in Leeds, she saw Gerry twice, but it was a busy time of year for him and she had the feeling that the friendship would gradually drop away. Apart from that, she was pleased to discover that Gerry had taken on an assistant at the riding school for the summer months, and his conversation seemed to include a lot about the new Vicky. Anna found herself being hopeful for Gerry's sake that he might have found someone who could share his interests and return his affection.

*   *   *

It was one day during a July heatwave that Anna returned from the studios, hot and weary and longing for a shower, and saw, with a shock, that there was a man standing outside her front door who looked like Paul. He was so often in her thoughts that at first she wondered if she were imagining things, but as she parked the car, he came down the steps and seconds later, she found herself in his arms.

'Paul, what are you doing here? How did you know where to find me?'

'Anna, it's good to see you,' he said, looking as if he really meant it. 'It wasn't difficult to find you. I guessed you would have been in touch with Gerry, so I went to see him. Can I come in? I have something rather serious to say to you.'

She looked at him in some surprise. He sounded quite grim and there was a note of worry in his voice.

'Come in,' she said, 'and we'll take some drinks out into the garden.'

Anna was quite pleased with the results of her efforts in the garden; she had got the lawn under control and cleared the borders to find quite a lot of herbaceous plants, now bright with colour.

As she sipped her drink, she looked at Paul, and she couldn't still the thudding of her heart. He seemed unusually solemn, yet reluctant to tell her what had brought him to Leeds. So she took the bull by the horns and asked him straight out.

'What's so serious that it's brought you all this way, Paul?'

In reply, he asked her a question. 'Did the police ever tell you of their investigations after the fire, Anna? Did they leave the case open?'

'The fire?' She was quite startled. She would never forget it, but as far as she was concerned, it was a thing of the past. 'They were quite honest with me,' she replied. 'They said they hadn't been able to find a single shred of evidence and they also said it was often the same in a close-knit community, especially one that was united in a common cause, as Stanton was against the tea-room. No-one had seen anything suspicious, no-one had seen anyone about late at night when the letters were delivered.

'The police were assuming that the letters and the fire were the work of one person because of the warning in the very last letter. They couldn't identify the handwriting on the envelopes either.' She looked at him. 'Paul, why are you asking me about it now? Has some evidence turned up or something?'

'Yes, I think it has,' he replied, 'but in rather a strange and unhappy way.' He was speaking very slowly and seemed upset.

'Whatever do you mean?' she asked. 'What's happened?'

'It's about Marcia, Anna.'

'Marcia?' She could do no more than echo a woman's name. So it was Marcia who was upsetting Paul.

'Yes, she has been ill. She's been taken to a special clinic and she's asking for you.'

Anna was dumbfounded. 'Asking for me? Why on earth would she ask for me? We weren't exactly on good terms.'

Paul took her hand and didn't seem to know that he was holding it very tightly. 'I arranged for her to go into the clinic for treatment. It's part of a psychiatric hospital. Marcia's suffering from some kind of paranoia— it's related to the depression she's been experiencing for years.'

Anna looked at him aghast. 'Paranoia? But, Paul, I thought that was something to do with delusions or being persecuted or something.'

'Yes, you're partly right and that's why I've come to see you.' He broke off and lifted her hand to his lips. 'I'm finding this very difficult, Anna. You see, Marcia has got it into her head that you're the cause of all her troubles and she seems to want to see you. I think I know what the problem is, but she hasn't been entirely open with me and I am only guessing at things. Oh, I'm sorry, Anna. I didn't want to upset you.'

Anna was bewildered. 'I just don't understand,' she said. 'I know you were going to marry Marcia and I'm sorry if she's been ill, but I don't see where I come into it, except— except for that time when she came in and warned me not to look in your direction.'

125

Paul spoke gently. 'Marcia was the one who told you I was going to marry her—not me. There's only one person I want to marry and it's not Marcia and never has been. But that can wait. What I have to ask you is this—for the sake of Marcia's sanity, would you be prepared to come to the hospital with me to see her? I would be with you all the time and she's not violent, so you needn't be afraid. Would you do it—to please me, Anna?'

Anna was silent for a long time, thinking of Marcia and thinking of the things that Paul had said. Then she made up her mind quickly.

'Yes, of course I will, Paul. Where is the hospital?'

'It's at Hawsley.'

'Oh, that's not very far out of Leeds. Have you been visiting her, Paul?'

'Yes, I have and I've seen her getting worse. That's what made me come to seek you out I don't think you'll regret going, Anna.' He suddenly smiled as though he was relieved that the ordeal of asking was over. 'Now, tell me about yourself and where you're working. I want to hear all about it and I want to take you out to dinner tonight. Will you come?'

Anna was relieved, too, at the change of subject and began to tell him of her new life and how she was waiting until Gable End was sold before buying a house of her own. The estate agent had told her that he had someone interested, but that no offer had yet been made.

Paul waited in the garden while Anna went to shower and change, then they headed towards Otley to a hotel that Paul knew well.

It was an entrancing evening for Anna. Paul forgot his worries over Marcia and they found themselves back with the same bond of intimacy and friendship, not spoiled by passion or emotion. They agreed to meet on Saturday to go to the hospital and Paul's kiss as he left her at the flat was soft and caring and somehow possessive . . .

CHAPTER TEN

They set off for Hawsley on the Saturday afternoon in pouring rain which seemed to add gloom to their already sober mood. Anna was feeling both nervous and apprehensive. She knew that Paul would be with her, but she was not looking forward to meeting an unpredictable Marcia Camberley. She had been intimidating enough before she was taken ill.

The hospital was set in pleasant grounds and Paul led Anna to a one-storeyed, modern block where she followed him to a large sitting-room with a french window opening on to lawns and bright flower beds.

Sitting near the window were a man and a

woman, and Anna felt a sense of hesitation in Paul at her side.

'Paul, it's nice of you to come.'

Anna recognised the voice, but when she looked at Marcia she hardly knew her. Her ex-neighbour had lost a lot of weight, her eyes were dark and haunted, and her hair was grey—she looked ten years older.

The man at her side was rising and Marcia's voice continued. 'Paul, I've got a nice surprise. This is my eldest brother, Alistair—he's come all the way from America to see me. Alistair, this is the Paul Buxton I've been telling you about, and with him is Anna Hadlee who used to live next door to me.'

Anna realised that Marcia's voice was pitched high and held a note of panic in it. They all shook hands and sat down together. In her own nervous way, Marcia seemed to be in control of the situation, which surprised Anna, who had expected her to be in more of a confused state.

Marcia was still speaking. 'Paul, I think Alistair is going to be the answer to all my problems. I'm going to go back to the States with him and he suggests that if I like it, I could settle there and buy a place near him and his wife, Millie. It's easy to get an analyst over there—everybody has one—and I think that's just what I need, don't you?'

'Yes, Marcia—I think it's a good idea,' Paul replied warmly.

'But, Paul.' Marcia paused for a moment but did not look at Anna. 'I'm glad you've brought Anna. My doctor has persuaded me that I must see her as I've got a lot to say to her.'

'Go on, Marcia,' Paul said gently.

In all the words and broken sentences that followed, Marcia did not once look at Anna, but spoke directly to Paul. And Anna listened, mesmerised, unable to believe the complexity of Marcia's mind and feelings.

'The moment Anna moved in next door she was a threat,' Marcia was saying. 'She hadn't been there more than ten minutes when she was worrying me about her burst pipes. But it was when she moved to Windhayes that I really started to worry. I knew she was bound to meet you and I didn't want her to. She was far too young and pretty for my liking. As for the tea-room idea, I didn't believe for a moment that she would get planning permission, but it served its purpose. I saw her with you, Paul, and then that day you were cross with me, you took her to Hatton Stacy. You had a good excuse because I had that awful headache, but I didn't trust her.'

Marcia stopped speaking and leaned closer to Paul and her voice was raised and shrill. 'I couldn't bear to lose you, Paul. I couldn't bear it, as you were my only friend; so I told her we were hoping to get married. I know you'd never mentioned that, but I always hoped,

Paul. I always hoped.'

Anna glanced at Paul's face; it was tight-lipped, his eyes hard, yet pitying at the same time. His hands were clenched, she noticed.

'So I had to put her off, didn't I? That's when I thought of getting at her through the tea-room idea. No-one in the village wanted it. You didn't want it, I didn't want it, so I had the idea of sending her the anonymous letters.'

Anna gasped out loud; Marcia had sent the letters! She had never for a moment suspected.

'It worked, too—for a time; she took up with that Gerry Pearson and I thought I was safe. Then I saw you with her. I was looking out of the window when the car drew up on the green. And you kissed her—I saw you kiss her. Then you came in to see me and we had that quarrel—I was sure you wanted to marry me, but I could see that you were turning to Anna and I had to work fast. I had to get her out of the way somehow. I thought about it all night. I would scare her away, but I did warn her. I put a note through the next morning. But she didn't know what was coming to her. She didn't know, did she?'

Marcia's voice was getting hysterical and they all seemed to be transfixed. Her brother put out a hand to her but she brushed it aside.

'No, I must finish. I saw her go out with Linda and knew it would be some time before she would be home. So I got a rag and soaked it in paraffin and crept next door. When the

130

rag was halfway through the letter-box, I put a match to it. No-one saw me. No-one saw me do it and the police didn't suspect me at all. I got away with it, didn't I?'

She turned, at last, to Anna, and her eyes were blazing with emotion. 'You went away, didn't you? I got rid of you and I had Paul to myself. Then I was ill and he was kind to me and he got me in here, but the nightmares wouldn't go away. I knew all the time you were going to find out and you would tell the police and I would be put in prison. Paul didn't know I set fire to your house—I didn't tell him. I've never talked about it before, not to anyone. So now you know the truth and I am going to America, so you can have Paul if you want him. They understand these things over there. So you can go now. I've told you the truth and if you go to the police, I won't be here. I'll be where they can't get me. I'm right, aren't I, Alistair?'

There was a deathly silence in the room, all eyes on the gaunt woman who had told her tragic story. It was Paul who spoke first.

'Marcia—'

'No, Paul, don't you say anything. Let me hear from Anna.' Marcia turned round. 'Are you going to the police? Are you?'

Anna felt a sick churning in her stomach, her eyes met Paul's and she didn't need the appeal she saw in them to tell her what she had to say. She got up and stood in front of

131

Marcia.

'Marcia, you were right in thinking I never suspected you. I can still hardly believe it, but I suppose it all makes sense. Marcia, if want you to know that, as far as I am concerned, it's all in the past now. Gable End will be sold and people will forget.' She stopped and then spoke slowly. 'No-one beyond this room will ever know the truth—it will go down as another unsolved crime. I'm very sorry that you're ill and hope you'll make a good recovery when you get to America.' Her voice faltered and she turned to make her way out of the room. 'I can't say any more. Goodbye.'

And she left them and ran to the carpark, standing in the pouring rain in front of the Jaguar.

Paul was there in minutes and held out his arms to her. She was glad to be taken close to him and she cried her heart out.

'Anna, we're getting soaked—into the car, quickly.' Paul's voice cut through Anna's tears and her sense of shock.

In the car, they threw their wet jackets on to the back seat and Anna sat quietly at Paul's side, his arm around her. He let the tumult of her thoughts subside before he spoke.

'Anna, thank you.'

She looked up at him, her eyes silently questioning.

'Thank you for what you said to Marcia and for deciding not to go to the police.'

'Oh, Paul,' she said, still with a sob in her voice, 'how could I? Poor Marcia. I never liked her, you know, but I hadn't realised how ill she was. I couldn't—I didn't understand how you came to like her so much, Paul. Oh, I'm sorry, I shouldn't say that—'

His hand stroked her wet hair. 'It's all right, my dear girl. I'll tell you the whole story of Marcia one day. It's tragic, but I think the move to America might be her salvation.'

'Did you know her brother was going to be there?' Anna asked.

'No, it was a complete surprise to me. She's often mentioned him, but it's been years since she's seen him. He seems a nice man and he's obviously very concerned about her if he's come straight over unannounced.'

Paul's fingers gripped her shoulder. 'Now, I want to suggest something, Anna, and I want you to put that last scene behind you. How would it do if I drove you back to your flat and you packed a bag and came to stay with me at Stanton for the week-end?'

'In your house?' There was surprise in Anna's voice.

'Yes, in my house. You've stayed there before, you know—only it was snowing that time!'

Anna laughed. 'Oh, Paul, I would like to. It'll help me to put Marcia out of my mind. I think I would have brooded about it all week-end.'

'Off we go then. We'll pack up your things and we can be in Stanton-le-Moor in just over an hour.'

As Anna saw the last of the buildings of Leeds slipping past and the landscape giving way to fields and woods, she felt a contented bubble of happiness building up inside her.

In the past, Paul had said many things that had made her ponder and she could not be sure of his intentions, but there was one thing she was certain of now and that was that he was never going to marry Marcia. She couldn't feel any hatred towards Marcia for what she had done—it was more a sense of pity and sadness. She wondered if Paul would ever tell her the background of the tragedy of Marcia's life and of how he had come to know her.

It was a heavenly feeling, knowing that she was travelling in the direction of Esterdale and although Paul had very little to say, as though his mind was still back in the hospital, he did give her occasional glances that encompassed her happiness and made her feel at one with him.

Anna discovered the name of his house for the first time as they turned into the drive— Stanton Grange. On her previous visit, the board had been hidden in the snow and she had never thought to ask. She rather liked the name—it seemed to describe exactly the low, rambling but elegant building that was neither house nor cottage.

As he carried her overnight bag to the front door, Paul looked down at her.

'Welcome to Stanton Grange,' he said, then gave her a grin which she was happy to see on his face. 'You didn't get much of a welcome the last time you were here, did you?'

She laughed up at him. 'It was hardly surprising. It is lovely to be back in mid-summer—even if it is pouring. Thanks for asking me.'

'I think food is the first priority. Why don't we have an early dinner at five o'clock—will that suit you? We'll make a pot of tea now, to keep us going.'

Anna wondered when he was going to mention Marcia again and she did not have long to wait. They went into the lounge and sat by the window looking out on to teeming rain and the drenched flowers and shrubs of the back garden. Paul broached the subject while Anna was pouring out the tea.

'Anna, I want to talk to you about Marcia. There's a lot you don't understand and if I tell you now then we needn't mention it again.'

'I was hoping you'd tell me, Paul, but I didn't like to ask.'

'I've known her a long time,' he said, 'over ten years in fact. She married a great friend of mine and although I didn't really take to her— she was rather formidable even in those days— I was prepared to accept her as Christopher's wife. I thought they were rather ill-suited, but

135

they seemed to be devoted and when Marcia found she was expecting a baby, their happiness was complete.' He stopped, his thoughts and memories obviously back in the past.

'The next part is very hard to tell. I was manager of a hotel near Chester at the time and they were on their way up from the south to stay for a few days. They were in a bad accident on the motorway. Christopher was killed outright, Marcia was badly injured and she lost the baby.'

'Oh, Paul, poor Marcia! How dreadful,' Anna exclaimed.

He nodded. 'I don't think she ever got over it. I never lost touch with her and when she eventually settled in Stanton-le-Moor—and I think she chose it to be near me—I started to see quite a lot of her. There was never anything other than friendship in it, but as she got more and more neurotic, she also got more possessive towards me.

'I never loved her and neither did I have any intention of marrying her, in spite of what she liked to think and what she told you. Things weren't easy between us when you came on the scene, but I still supported her for Christopher's sake. I felt it was the least I could do—to offer her friendship, I mean.'

'But, Paul—' Anna started than stopped. She couldn't ask the question.

He looked at her. 'You want to know if I

knew about the letters and the fire?'

'Yes—I—'

'I didn't know, but I had my suspicions. Certain things didn't add up—her extreme jealousy of you for no reason at all; the fact that the letters just seemed to appear—no-one ever saw the person who put them through your letter-box. I thought that seemed to point to the culprit being someone living very near.'

'But the fire, Paul—' Anna felt she had to interrupt.

'I know—after the fire I thought I had been mistaken. I couldn't believe that Marcia would do a thing like that. But now I know I was wrong.'

There was a pause.

'Did you know what she was going to say today?' Anna asked at last.

He shook his head. 'No, I didn't know, but none of it came as a surprise. I'd seen her getting worse and worse and believed that her feelings of guilt could be the only reason. She had this unreasonable fear of you which should have vanished when you moved away from Stanton-le-Moor—but even when she was in the hospital having treatment, she still had the greatest resentment against you. That's why I risked everything to take you there. I hope you can forgive me. She said what I expected her to say, and you, bless you, were forgiving. If you really do mean to take it no further, I think that Marcia will have every chance of a good recovery once she's in America. It was the greatest good fortune that her brother should have arrived just at that moment.'

'Oh, Paul, I'm glad you told me everything and it's not a question of forgiveness. It means I can put it all right out of my mind now—it was an unhappy time, but perhaps some good will come out of it. I'll concentrate on earning my living for a few years and perhaps one day I'll be able to buy a little house somewhere in Esterdale.'

Anna looked up at Paul as he took both her hands in his.

'I don't suppose you'd like to concentrate on me for a change, would you?'

'Paul!'

He laughed aloud and it was good to hear the sound. Then he jumped up and pulled her to her feet. 'It's time to think about dinner now—afterwards, I'll take you up on the moor and we'll talk some more. We've got a lot of talking to do, young Anna.'

'I'm not all that young, Paul Buxton,' she said defensively.

'Seven years younger than I am,' he replied, then added with a joke in his voice. 'Perhaps that's just right.'

They cooked the meal together and Paul insisted on eating in the dining-room. Anna would have preferred to have eaten informally in the kitchen, but in the mood she was in, she was prepared to fall in with anything Paul suggested. They were comfortable together and she wanted to enjoy the harmony.

As they drove out of Stanton Grange and down the narrow lane that wound its way through endless miles of green fields before it reached the moor, the rain had cleared and a pale sun was low in the sky, casting long shadows at the group of trees where Paul stopped the car.

'This is one of my favourite walks,' Paul said. He had taken her hand in his and was striding along as though glad to be released into the open space and the freshness of the evening air. 'We'll go as far as that standing stone you can see over there. Can you make it that far?'

'Of course I can,' Anna replied, with some objection to the doubt about her walking ability. 'I walked a lot when I lived in Stanton.'

He laughed. 'Oh, yes, of course—I was forgetting the great trek to Brompton-in-Fenbydale. You were glad to see me that day, weren't you, Anna?'

She agreed with him happily, then looked rather sober and apologetic. 'I'm sorry we had so many disagreements over the tea-room, Paul. You must have been pleased when I decided to give up the idea and move back to Leeds.'

She was surprised at his reply.

'No, I wasn't pleased, Anna, it was taking

you away from me.'

'But I thought . . .?'

'You thought I had Marcia, and I thought you had Gerry. Well, we were both mistaken, weren't we?'

'Gerry was a good friend to me,' Anna said defensively.

'Yes—I thought he was too good a friend, but I know otherwise now.'

'Do you, Paul?' she asked.

'I had my eyes opened in no uncertain fashion when I went to ask him for your address. He told me he'd been to see you, then he introduced me to Vicky. It was very interesting. You could almost hear the wedding bells ringing!'

'Oh, Paul, I had a suspicion that things were going that way when he told me about her. I was so pleased. I never loved him, you know.'

He stopped in his tracks and looked down at her with a quizzical look in his eyes. 'So you are heart-whole, are you, Anna Hadlee?'

A glint of mischief appeared in her eyes and she was smiling at him. 'No, I wouldn't quite say that, Paul.'

'And does this have anything to do with it?' he asked, and without giving her a chance to reply, he drew her to him; his mouth was on hers and he was releasing a passion and a love which left her in no doubt about his feelings, and certainly confirmed in herself the love she had felt for him for a long time.

'Anna,' he murmured against her hair, still holding her tightly against him. 'I have loved you for a very long time. I love you, do you hear? I was going to ask you to marry me once before, but you gave me the shock of telling me what Marcia had said to you and then there was the fire and you moved away. But I told you that there was only one girl I wanted to marry and that girl was you. Are you going to tell me you love me? Are you going to tell me you will marry me? I'm waiting to hear the words, Anna.'

Anna listened to what he was saying with a sense of wonder. She knew now she had loved him since their very first kiss in the snow, but so many things had got in the way. So many misunderstandings had spoiled things for them.

Now he was giving her the chance to tell him of her true feelings.

She looked into his eyes and saw the pleading look of love. She couldn't tease him any more. There was only one thing she could say.

'I do love you, Paul. I love you very much.'

'And you will marry me?'

She put her arms right round him and buried her head against his chest and his answer came with a muffled laugh of delight.

'Oh, yes, Paul, I want to marry you above all things.'

They clung to each other and did not notice

that the sun had disappeared behind the western hills.

It was Paul who spoke first. 'And will you be quite happy living at Stanton Grange? You won't yearn for the city lights?'

She shook her head. 'Far from it. After I'd lived in Esterdale, I longed to be back here again—there's nowhere quite like it. You feel like that, too, don't you, Paul?'

'Yes, I do. There are so many things we have in common, Anna—we found that out straight away, didn't we?'

'After you'd stopped being furious with me,' she said with a grin.

'I'm sorry, you were the last straw that day. But it didn't stop me falling headlong in love with you.'

'That very day?' she asked, disbelieving.

'I'll tell you the truth—I fell in love with a beautiful and charming girl wearing my sweater and desperately trying to hold up my trousers round her waist.'

Anna couldn't stop laughing. 'Oh, Paul, you couldn't possibly have done. You're talking nonsense.'

He kissed her fiercely to prove his point and then they made their way back to the car.

'We'll go back by way of the village, just to have a look and lay any ghosts, shall we?' he asked her.

'Yes, I think I'd like that,' she replied.

In Stanton-le-Moor, they stopped on the

green and Anna looked at Gable End with its For Sale sign and gave a sigh.

'What's that for?' Paul asked her.

'It would have made a nice tea-room; wouldn't it?' she said dreamily.

Paul grabbed her and kissed her hard. 'Don't let me ever hear you mention that word again. Such things are not for Stanton-le-Moor.'

She giggled. 'I know, I know. But I wonder who'll live there? It was always such a happy house.'

He put an arm round her and gave her a gentle hug then whispered in her ear. 'I'll let you into a secret. You know the buyer that your agent told you was interested? I happen to know who it is and I think you're going to be very pleased.'

'Paul, what do you mean? How can you possibly know?'

'Listen, then, though I'm betraying a confidence. Michael is going to buy Gable End and he's hoping Linda will marry him and it'll be their home.'

Anna's eyes were like stars. 'Oh, that's wonderful—I always knew she liked him a lot. It's all good news—Gerry and Vicky—and Michael and Linda—it's the perfect happy ending.'

He took her in his arms. 'And don't forget, Paul and Anna,' he murmured. 'That really is a happy ending.'

We hope you have enjoyed this Large Print book. Other Chivers Press or Thorndike Press Large Print books are available at your library or directly from the publishers.

For more information about current and forthcoming titles, please call or write, without obligation, to:

Chivers Press Limited
Windsor Bridge Road
Bath BA2 3AX
England
Tel. (01225) 335336

OR

G.K. Hall & Co.
295 Kennedy Memorial Drive
Waterville
Maine 04901
USA

All our Large Print titles are designed for easy reading, and all our books are made to last.